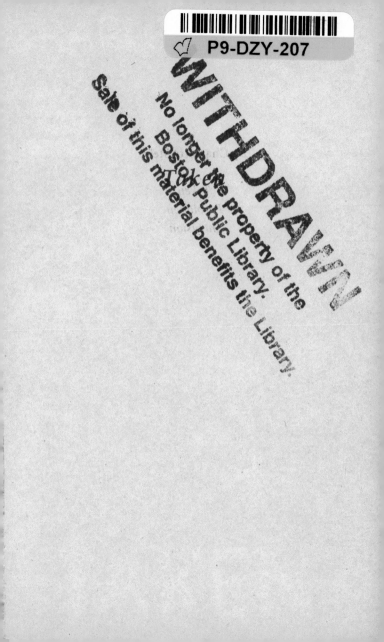

By Charlotte Stein

Taken
Forbidden
Intrusion

Taken

AN UNDER THE SKIN NOVEL

CHARLOTTE STEIN

red

AVON
IMPULSE

An Imprint of HarperCollins Publishers

TAKEN. Copyright © 2015 by Charlotte Stein. All rights reserved under International and Pan-American Copyright Conventions. By payment of the required fees, you have been granted the nonexclusive, nontransferable right to access and read the text of this e-book on screen. No part of this text may be reproduced, transmitted, decompiled, reverse-engineered, or stored in or introduced into any information storage and retrieval system, in any form or by any means, whether electronic or mechanical, now known or hereafter invented, without the express written permission of HarperCollins e-books.

EPub Edition APRIL 2015 ISBN: 9780062365125

Print Edition ISBN: 9780062365132

AM 10 9 8 7 6 5 4 3 2

For my wolf

Chapter One

THE WHOLE IDEA is hers. I want nothing to do with it, and not just because I hate the thought of wrecking all those nice books and doing something so bad. There is also the person we are doing this to: the strange guy who owns this creaking, quiet little store. The one I call the secret werewolf in my head—because honestly, that is what he looks like. He wears tweedy jackets with leather elbow patches and these tiny, wire-rimmed glasses, so he should seem harmless. But then you notice his black-as-pitch beard and his wild, dark hair and his eyes like twelve past midnight, and suddenly it doesn't feel that way at all.

And especially when he's standing right over you, shouting about you touching his books. That's what made Marnie mad in the first place—he yelled at her for messing with the first-editions section—but mad is not the emotion I feel about the whole thing. Scared is more how I would describe my reaction. My heart tried to eat itself when he strode out from between the stacks, twice as tall as any other guy I know and so burly it kind of shocked me.

Rare-book store owners are not supposed to be burly.

But he definitely is.

I can see one of his arms from where we are currently standing, despite the fact that he is at the other end of the store and we are hidden by shelves as tall and gnarly as trees in a haunted forest. That limb just makes itself visible by being completely massive, to the point where I am starting to sweat. If he sees Marnie pulling books off shelves, she is going to be in so much trouble. *I* am going to be in so much trouble.

And as for starting a fire…

"What are you doing?" I snap because seriously this was not what we discussed. She said she was just going to come in here and do a bit of mischief, not burn the goddamn place down. I thought she meant creasing the corner on page seven of *War and Peace,* and to be honest, even that was too far for me. The books in here are absolutely gorgeous. The owner might be a maniac. It all seemed like the very worst thing in the world.

And then she starts in on actual arson.

Oh God, she plans to commit arson.

"I told you: teaching him a lesson," she says, and I can see it in her hand.

A can of lighter fluid that she's getting ready to spray.

"This is not a lesson, Marnie. This is suicide."

"No way, you think that pompous jackass is going to do anything? He's not going to do anything, and besides, we can be out the door before he even knows."

"The door is past where he is right now."

"Yeah, but I bet he's superslow."

"I don't think he's slow, Marnie," I say, but even I have no real idea how right I am about that. I picture him lumbering after us as we dash down the street. I think of him sort of catching me as I round the shoe place on the corner. I do not expect him to be so quick that he comes up on us before we even know he has moved. That is not just fast. That is pretty much superhuman and insanely stealthy. For a second I think something mad like *did he take off his shoes to do it?*

And then all my thoughts are cut off at the knees.

They have to be, because oh my God he just grabbed me. I swear to God he *grabs* me. His enormous arms go right around my middle, and not in a simple and straightforward restraining sort of way. He actually lifts me clean off the ground. I see both of my feet kick up in an arc, those cute purple Converse suddenly so small and silly seeming. I should have chosen something more adult, I know, and now I am going to be murdered while wearing them. Someone will find one in the gutter three months from now, and it will serve as a sad indictment of our times. A guy on CNN will say that girls should go out only in proper shoes.

Then no one will ever speak of me again.

Not even Marnie, who has already apparently fled. I glance around in terror, half hoping she will come at him with a baseball bat. But no, she is completely and utterly gone without so much as a panicked good-bye. There is just me and this guy, battling it out.

Only "battling" implies I have some sort of shot at this, when really I have none at all. His arms are not only enormous but seemingly made of steel. I try to push against them and get absolutely nowhere. If anything they only get tighter around me, which is definitely a bad thing. I can hardly breathe as it is. Any more of this and I might pass out, and if I do God only knows what could happen. Most likely I will wake up in a sex den, sold by the secret werewolf to pay for more rare books.

It even sounds like a story I heard on true crime stories.

Or maybe while watching the movie *Taken*.

Either way I have to stay conscious. I have to stay calm. He is probably not going to do anything bad to me, after all. He probably just wants to hurl me out of the store, I tell myself, but of course that only makes it worse when I see the front window receding from view. I watch it go like a long-lost friend, realization slowly and painfully dawning on me. He is not taking me out.

He is taking me toward the back of the store.

Toward a door like something out of all my nightmares, narrow and gnarled and covered in thick maroon paint. It looks like it would probably fit well in a movie made by Dario Argento, and I see when he somehow manages to open it that I am right. The stairs beyond it go straight down to hell. I last saw them while watching *The Evil Dead*, only these are steeper and starker and so much more frightening—most probably because I go down them while being carried by another person. Going down stairs while being carried is eight hundred times more vertigo inducing than doing it on your own.

I almost vomit before we get to the bottom.

But that might be more because of what this means. He really is going to do something horrid to me, I think. This is what being held hostage feels like. This is the thing that happens before women are horribly brutalized in dank basements, and it is happening to *me*. The only difference is that the basement in question is not exactly dank. There is a bed with a neatly crocheted bedspread and a record player on a stand in the corner. The lamp on the chest of drawers by the far wall is a kind of Tiffany's-looking thing, so the light is just as cozy as can be and so welcoming you could almost imagine sitting down to have tea.

Though to be honest, all of that only makes it worse. This could be his nice little nest, where he does his evil deeds in comfort. He probably has a day planner some-where detailing when and where he plans on snatching another one—only *I* am the other one. I am his *seven-teenth* victim; nasty, trashy Rosie Callahan, who almost definitely had it coming.

God, the news is going to say I had it coming. They will find my mom in some casino somewhere and have her cry about how I never called and left her all alone to go to a third-rate college and now probably sleep with a ton of guys. And the thing is, none of that is wrong exactly. Those surface details are all accurate. I *did* leave her all alone and my college *is* third rate and I *have* slept with a ton of guys.

But sleeping with a ton of guys does not mean I deserve to be murdered.

Sadly for me, however, that is definitely what is going to happen. There was a slim chance it wouldn't, somewhere at the top of the stairs. And even when we get down there, I think I might still escape. But then I feel something cool and steely snap around my wrist, and I pretty much know it's game over.

What else could it be, when he just handcuffed me?

He handcuffed me to a length of chain that leads to the bed frame—a move that could have been made only by a man who wants to do me wrong. There is no other explanation now. No loophole I can get through. All I can do is plead with him, but when I do, something strange happens. "Just let me go, okay, let me go; don't hurt me," I say, and he immediately steps away.

He steps so far back he almost passes into the place next door—though that isn't really the thing that gives me pause. He might have a weird thing with his victims, where he doesn't want to touch them too much right away. Maybe emotions make him feel weird, and he has to wait until all the tears have drained out of me to do his foul business.

His going over there could mean nothing.

But his expression is another story. His eyebrows are almost in his hair. It seems like he wants to say something, but has no idea what the something might be.

And his hands...

I cannot overlook his panicked hands. He has them spread in the universally accepted gesture for *calm down* or maybe *no, wait a minute*, and he does it in so sincere a way I find myself suddenly 70 percent less fearful. The tears that were coming in a flood slow to a trickle, and they stop altogether when he finally speaks.

"This is not what this is. Is that what it looks like this is? Like I might hurt you? I just wanted to keep you here until the cops came. I had no idea that…oh my God. Oh my God, I have…I need to just go upstairs for a second…" he says, and then I get this enormous rush of total relief. Or at least I do until it gets to an hour later, down here in the basement of doom.

And still no secret werewolf.

I THINK I start shouting at around four thirty in the afternoon. It could be later or earlier, though. My phone died on me twenty minutes before I walked in the store, and apparently that was my only access to the passage of time. I guess you realize you stopped wearing a watch only when it really matters. And care about your battery only when you think you will never, ever be held hostage for committing arson.

Though I go back-and-forth on whether that has really happened. After a while I start wondering if he just died of a heart attack at the top of the stairs—though even if he did I can see that this does not exactly help me. If anything, it makes everything way, way worse. Now not only am I chained to a bed in a bookstore basement, I am chained to a bed with no hope of ever getting released. At the very least there was a medium chance of that happening before.

If he died, there could well be none.

I might be here for days.

I could possibly pee myself—or worse. Maybe this is like that *Hitchcock* episode I saw as a kid where the woman voluntarily gets buried alive to escape prison, and then she strikes a match and sees the man who was supposed to get her out buried next to her. He never meant to leave me down here to die. But since he himself is a corpse, he can't exactly help me.

All of which sounds insane, I know.

But it still makes me shout louder. I yell things like *hey, there is a person down here*, and just pray that the coroner hears me before he clears the dead werewolf away. Is it a coroner in situations like this? Somehow I suspect I have it wrong, but sue me—I am stuck in a basement. My mind is not real clear on crime scene etiquette right now. Most of it is just focusing on getting someone's attention.

Even if the someone in question is the secret werewolf.

And he seems superannoyed once I have said attention. He comes stomping down the stairs like I am the worst person in the world for wanting to be free, and demands to know what I think I am doing. "Stop making such a racket," he says, as though I'm a kid he offered to babysit instead of his prisoner. Honestly it has to be the weirdest thing anyone has ever done in front of me before, yet strangely it doesn't feel that way. It feels like he is fully justified in that bizarre response.

I actually struggle to contradict him, which kind of makes me worry that this is how Stockholm syndrome starts. Your captor is so baffled and exasperated about things that you find it hard to believe he might be wrong. Mostly I just want to laugh or maybe spend a lot of time marvelling over his amazing beard—both of which seem wrong for this sort of situation.

So I do my best to be as tough as possible.

"You just chained me up in your basement. Why on earth would I want to stay quiet?" I say, and for good measure I rattle the handcuffs at him. However, I do not get the answer I expect. I doubt anyone could expect this answer, considering he delivers it in a kind of helpless tone most typically reserved for people who just realized their brake line has been cut and the oncoming train is not stopping.

"Because I think I might have accidentally kidnapped someone, and when you shout it makes me want to die of disgust at myself. Plus the chances of me going to prison go up a *whole hell of a lot*."

He barely takes a breath through the whole sentence.

But that's okay; I barely take a breath after it.

He really did not intend any of this. It was all just a mistake, done in the heat of the moment. The only problem is—the heat of the moment is currently becoming an actual solid issue, in a way I can just about understand. If he gets the police now to arrest me for arson, chances are they might wonder why I am in this basement. This scary basement, that looks a little like a serial killer's lair. And one word from me…

"Dude, honestly you have nothing to worry about. I will never say anything."

"Despite the fact that you hate me so much you tried to burn down my store."

"That was all my friend—not even my friend, really. More of an acquaintance."

"So you wanted nothing to do with any of it. I just spent an hour realizing I could not call the cops for nothing."

"No, not even a tiny thing. I would never. I think you're cool, honestly," I say, and feel sure that will settle it. Or at least I do until I see the rising concern all over his face. It starts around the eyebrows and progresses over his face like the dawning of a new day. And when he speaks, just about the same thing happens. He starts out almost calm and ends in a kind of despairing panic.

"Oh my God, are you trying to bargain for your freedom? You are. You are trying to persuade me to let you go. You're practically begging me. Holy crap, you're begging me. This is the worst thing I have ever done. They will be fully justified in putting me away for a thousand years," he says. He even puts his hands in his hair.

Clearly, I am not handling this well.

Really though, can anyone blame me? In ordinary situations I tend to not cope. The last exam I took, I spent all night before it eating Peeps and watching episode after episode of a show I barely like, then slept through my alarm and had to go to it wearing a towel on my head. It is literally a miracle that I am thinking rationally or talking at all in light of this—so much of a miracle, in fact, that I start to feel a little weirded out about it. Is it just his strange affability that makes me calm?

Or is it something inside me?

It feels like it might be something inside me. Like that time when I was a kid and we found a bobcat under the porch and Susie Sylvester said "I dare you to." Or when no one else would jump and grab the rope over the lake. Or when Marnie said, "Hey, you want to go get that guy back for being a total asshole?" And I should have said no. I should have all three times, I *should* have. I had to have rabies shots and I almost drowned and now I might be an arsonist.

All of it ends with me hurt.

But oh man the pain is so sweet.

"They won't put you away for a thousand years—look at me, I look like a punk," I say, then for good measure I show him the tattoo I got not so long ago, of a snake eating itself around my right wrist. The one that I oddly want him to see, despite the thing it really proves. That I probably was up to no good. I did want to burn down his store. I am a bad person, and he should be angry with me.

I wonder if he will grab me again if he gets angry.

I wonder if he will do it from the front so I can look at his beard while he does it.

And when he makes it clear that this will never happen, something weird happens.

"Fuck no, you are as cute as a button, the cutest thing I have ever seen, so cute and so *young*. Christ, I'm starting to feel queasy about how young you are," he says, and then I think like some insane reflex:

Dammit no, I am *a disaster and* definitely *of an appropriate age.*

Though the question remains: an appropriate age for *what*?

"I will totally be twenty-four in June."

"That does not make it better. Did you think that saying it would make it better?"

"Well…yeah I mean what are you like…thirty?"

"I was thirty around four hundred years ago. This is a *nightmare*," he says, but apparently my brain does not agree. He says *four hundred years* and I swear to God I go all funny and tingly, as though agedness is a sexy thing now. I would probably start worrying I had unresolved Daddy issues, if he looked anything like my father. But as my father was a tiny accountant with a face like a fuzzy peach, I think I might be in the clear.

And besides, he doesn't *really* look four hundred.

He just looks big and hairy and rugged, like he spends his spare time climbing mountains in the dark, or was possibly enslaved in the sixteenth century by his vampire betters. I bet he had a long-lost love who burned to death, leaving him tormented and lovelorn and oh my God I really need to stop thinking like this. It only makes things worse, in a way I would rather not look too deeply into.

Right now I need to be calm—and most of all: normal.

God, I wish I knew how to be normal.

"I really doubt it makes any difference how old you are."

"Sure it does. Gigantic Ancient Man Steals Tiny Kid is a way worse headline."

"Come on—you can hardly call me a kid. Or tiny, for that matter."

"You look pretty small to me. I bet I could circle your thigh with one hand."

"Yeah, that might be because your hands are enormous."

"Either way sounds bad. It sounds like I might need a Lifetime movie made about my reign of terror. I even have three weird names: Johann Wilhelm Weir."

"What difference do three weird names make?"

"All Lifetime movie serial killers have three weird names," he says, which sounds so scary I know I should finally feel it. I know I should, but he just does it so matter-of-factly I find it impossible to. He sounds almost like he's telling me about the dry cleaners being closed when he went to pick up that outfit he needs for a wedding. He even spreads his hands and shakes his head, like *huh, typical right?*

And then there is the other thing.

"And what if I think those names are cool?"

"You do *not* think my names are cool."

"They could well be the coolest names I've ever heard."

"But they sound so old. So old and so *German*," he says, and I gotta be honest. I love how he does it. I love that he makes that last word into some kind of curse, as though some witch laid it on him a hundred years ago and now he has to bear its terrible weight.

He periodically wants to wear lederhosen and eats bratwurst by the barrel.

"The German thing is what makes them awesome."

"Now I know you're screwing with me. Either that or trying to flatter me to get out of this—which by the way is even worse than begging for your life. You should not have to say nice things to get out of this. It is way worse if you have to say nice things to get out of this. I will probably get beat up in prison, if I'm not somehow mysteriously killed in the squad car on the way to the station first."

"Well, before you are, could you just maybe speak a little of it for me?"

"Speak a little of what exactly? What are we talking about here?"

"We were talking about the German that you might possibly speak."

"I thought we were talking about me holding you against your will then being arrested and murdered in a police car, after which there will be a Lifetime movie based on my life called *Ugly Hairy Guy Held Me Hostage: The Whatever Your Name Is Story*," he says, and then a giggle just pops right out of me. Can you blame me, though?

I think he might be the funniest person I've ever met, and not just because of the things he comes out with. It's the *delivery* of the things. The combination of completely laid-back and sort of wired at the same time—which sounds impossible, I know.

But he makes it work.

"My name is Rosie Callahan."

"So basically the most adorable name ever. Fits right in there perfectly. I bet they will get Zooey Deschanel wearing a pink dress to play you."

"You think I look like Zooey Deschanel?" I ask, and in response he immediately backs up three paces. He holds up his hands, as though I accused him of a sex crime.

"Absolutely not, no way, how could I possibly when I have never for one second considered your appearance in any way whatsoever, I swear, Your Honor," he says, after which I just cannot help it. I have to really laugh—partly because my fear is gone but mostly because he really is just fucking hilarious.

Seriously, have I ever known anyone as hilarious as him?

"Why are you laughing? This is not funny. This is creepy."

"You want to laugh too—I can totally tell."

"I do *not*. This is really serious," he says, even though I think he agrees. For a second he looks almost relaxed. He shakes his head at me and huffs out this faintly disbelieving sort of sound. It even looks like he might sit down, and then after he has I could really settle in too. We could just be two people having the most amazing conversation there has ever been—because honestly I have never in my life spoken to anyone like this. I had no idea I could get along with someone in this way. I thought I was doomed to have stilted chats with people about things I care nothing about until the end of time. I was sure that was the way things were, until *this*.

The only thing I need to do now is forget that *this* is some kind of hostage situation—though oddly I am kind of wondering if that is some sort of secret ingredient. The thing that makes it easier or better or just something I can't quite put my finger on.

And then the bell rings upstairs and suddenly I know for sure.

I feel it thrill through me, just like when I ran out to that rope.

When the stakes are higher, everything is heightened. Everything comes fiercer and faster and all in a tumble, even words you never knew you wanted to speak and things you never knew you felt. That buzzer goes and our eyes practically lock. And though he says, "You see how serious this is?"

I think he wants to tell me something else instead.

Something desperate, something that makes my heart hum.

"I know. I could totally scream for help."

"And you would have every right to."

"So you wouldn't try to stop me?"

"Of course not. I could never."

"No hand over my mouth."

"Christ no—no way."

"Not even for a second," I say, and I could swear on a stack of Bibles that something odd passes between us when I do. A kind of frisson or an understanding that I can barely grasp. All I know is I see him doing it so clearly—two big steps and he would be on me, one hand pressing tight to keep all my words in and the other somewhere else that I won't think about right now—and when I do I get the strangest sensation. I think *he* gets the strangest sensation. As soon as it happens, his face seems to sink. His eyes widen and his hands make fists and oh my God oh my God what *is* this?

I have no clue, but think he somehow might.

I think that's why he shakes his head, real slow.

"Not even if you wanted me to," he says, but somehow that only makes it worse. It introduces a new and completely insane concept: *me wanting*.

Even though that cannot possibly be a thing. I was scared not so long ago. I should be scared now. Nothing has changed—aside from the suggestion of choice. I mean he did just suggest *choosing*, didn't he? And if he did I have to wonder:

What sort of person would choose *yes*?

"And I guess that would be pretty weird of me."

"That would be very weird of you."

"Not like a normal person."

"Maybe not."

"But maybe…"

"Maybe normal is a little overrated," he says, but as soon as he does he looks like he might have made a huge mistake. He shakes himself as though waking from a dream, and holds up his hands like I shoved my shoulder against his defenses, and when he speaks it doesn't come out right. His sentence has holes in it, as though I poked them with a fork.

"I better…go…see what they…" he says, but really it isn't the fact that I could strain my food through those few words that makes me think he is afraid.

It's the way he runs for the stairs and takes them two at a time.

Chapter Two

HE IS QUICKER about coming back this time, but probably not because he is supereager to see me. He seems even more unsettled than he did when he left, and especially when he takes in the thing that I've been doing in his absence. In fact for the longest time he just stares at me as though I am a ghost. The ghost of recently deceased normality, I think it might be, because even I know this is strange.

For a start, I'm lying on the bed where I was meant to meet my demise, one ankle crossed over the other like this is some kind of insane summer camp.

And to finish, there is this little factoid:

"Are you seriously reading my book?"

Honestly I doubt he could have sounded more incredulous if he had caught me stark naked astride an emu. I have to check to make sure this isn't secretly his diary—but no, not even close. For some bizarre but completely okay-for-me-to-be-reading reason he was enjoying one of the Sookie Stackhouse books. He has even underlined a passage in careful pencil that I will most likely remember for all eternity.

I want to call you all those gooshy words you use when you love someone, no matter how stupid it sounds.

"I had to pass the time somehow."

"So you thought you would just make yourself comfortable."

"I could writhe in agony if that would make you feel better."

"Okay, I am just going to skip right over *that* one," he says, and oh man, I love the way he does it. I can hardly explain why, however. There is just the quality to him, this laconic, literal quality that no one I know possesses. I never even knew it was possible to be the way he is. Everyone in my life is tightly closed and completely false by comparison, which just makes me regret it even more when he adds: "And I can because I am now going to let you go. See here—keys."

Though I try not to show it.

It seems bonkers enough as it is, without him making some comment about it like: *you know you're supposed to feel happy about that, right? Happiness is the thing where you smile and then run and tell the police that a maniac is running a store in the city.* Because bizarrely I know he would. I can hear his timing and everything, after five minutes in his company. I can even see the way he would probably look at me.

With lots of eyebrow and those black eyes over the top of his glasses.

Christ, I need to not think about those black eyes over the top of his glasses. When he sits cautiously next to me on the bed to unlock the cuffs, I get to see far too much of them up close. And what I see is not comforting to me. Instead I have to deal with things that make my hairs bristle like: *he seems to have no pupils.*

That's how dark his eyes are. They devour his pupils.

And the energy in his gaze…

I wish I could explain it. It feels like he is vibrating somewhere just beneath the surface of his bookseller skin. Like he might rip it off at any moment and reveal his crazy plan for safecracking the pawn shop down the street or stealing motorbikes from the dealers on Maple Street and taking off for Texas.

I can almost picture myself on the back of one of them.

Which is most likely why I say what I do.

"Is it really a good idea to let me go?"

"I think it might be the best idea ever."

"I could still get you into a lot of trouble," I say, then immediately regret it. The whole concept of wanting to stay makes sense only in my head, where I am currently busy riding off with him on the back of a stolen Harley. He has no idea about any of that. He just thinks I am a total and utter weirdo who wants to stay kidnapped in a basement.

And it shows on his face.

And in his awesome words.

"Let's be honest: I *deserve* trouble for this. Now hold out that wrist—I think the key is this little red one. Or maybe the little blue one. Guess now we find out," he says, at which point his matter-of-factness moves up a notch from interesting to kind of exciting. Is exciting okay for it to be? It seems to not make any sense at all, but nothing I do will stop it.

He's busy trying to fit a key into a lock, and I'm grinning at him like a lunatic.

"You know I am never going to really, right? You're like the nicest guy in the world."

"How do you figure that one? I'm here unchaining you."

"Exactly. You're unchaining me," I say, and I do my best to push the significance of that concept, I really do.

But he just gives me this one weary laugh and shakes his head.

He *loves* shaking his head, and has about a million ways of doing it.

This one I call: *man, you are a card.*

"Hey—this is the bare minimum of decency."

"Even though I vandalized your store."

"That still doesn't excuse kidnapping."

"I think *kidnapping* is a little strong at this point."

"I don't. I shouldn't have done it. I want to not do things like this."

"So you've kidnapped girls before," I say, and the look he gives me is priceless.

It seems like an eyebrow raise, without any of his eyebrows going up.

I want to call it withering, but that seems too strong. And too not sexy.

"I mean crazy things in general, not specifically that one horrendous act."

"I think this was pretty far from a horrendous act."

"Not to me it wasn't."

"You didn't hurt me."

"That's your standard? Get a new one immediately. No one should ever hurt you because they have poor impulse control and a tendency toward bizarre random actions. Though I want to stress here I never hurt anyone because of that…issue. I just…did a lot of stupid things."

"Like ordering the wrong Margaret Atwood title for a customer," I say, sure that he knows I'm teasing him. In fact I think he does—the way he eyes me gives me goose pimples on my vagina. All of his facial hair just joins forces to send me straight to hell.

But he takes the bait anyway.

"Like doing time."

Most probably because he wants to shock me.

And it does—just maybe not in the way he intended.

I'm not scared straight, let's put it that way.

"You did *time*?"

"That's part of the reason I panicked, heinous actions aside. I have priors, man. I have a checkered past. They seriously could put me away for a thousand years."

"I *knew* you were a secret werewolf," I say, but only because I can't stop myself.

It just rams its way out of me before I can do anything about it.

And then I have to deal with the consequences.

"That does not sound like something you should be so excited about."

"Oh, come on, that has to be the coolest thing ever."

"The fact that I went to jail for running naked down Main Street is the coolest thing ever?"

"You *ran naked* down *Main Street*?" I ask, and I know I sound too excited about it.

I know because he pretty much tells me so.

"Please start reacting the way you are supposed to."

"You mean like a good, normal girl?"

"No, I mean like someone with any sort of self-preservation instinct."

"Naked running is hardly the frightening crime of the century."

"It is when you naked run after robbing a library," he says, then quite obviously expects *this* to be the deal breaker. He even stops searching through the keys for a second and sits back, nodding as though to say *yeah, that's right, I am that evil criminal.* Unfortunately for him, however, I sound even more stunned and thrilled when I answer him.

"You *robbed* a *library*."

"Stop emphasizing words!"

"I can't help it—your major crime is book thievery. I should have known."

"In my defense I was very poor due to being a directionless asshole and also I was extremely thirsty for literature."

He was thirsty for literature. Dear Lord, he had a *thirst* that he needed to *slake*.

I just want to do something mad like plunge my hands knee-deep in his rambling hair.

"Oh my God, this is the greatest thing I've ever heard. Why do you sound ashamed?"

"I owned a denim jacket with cut-off sleeves and *Han* written in studs on the back. I lived in a trailer and thought shoes were overrated. My favorite pastime aside from criminal reading was wearing a snake as a pair of pants. *That* is why I sound ashamed," he says, but the thing is he really believes it. He honestly imagines this is the icing on the crap cake, and now I get to spell it out for him.

"You called yourself Han as in short for Johann but also like Han Solo," I say, as though I can already see him soaring through the distant reaches of the galaxy at the helm of the *Millennium Falcon. Make that Kessel Run in twelve parsecs, baby,* I think at him.

And judging by his expression, he can totally tell.

"I kind of want to take that back now because even I can see it seems cool."

"Pretty much all of it is cool. You *so* are a secret werewolf."

"I will agree if secret werewolf is street lingo for reformed and repentant book lover."

"You know that isn't street lingo for any of that at all."

"Dare I ask what exactly it is?" he tries, so cautious I want to tease him again.

But the thing is: he has good reason to be. When I answer him my voice is all…quavery. I think I might be starting to seem like a kid with a crush, which even I can see is beyond bonkers. I barely know him. He is currently trying to undo the handcuffs he clapped on me. I should not be shivering every time the tip of his forefinger almost brushes my wrist as he presses a key to the lock. I should not hold my breath because the metal slides against the sensitive skin there every time he tentatively tries.

Yet that is exactly what is happening.

"You know—someone who's all hairy and wild under their bookish exterior."

"Okay, hairy is fair enough. I am exceedingly hairy. But I work on the wild part now, I really do. I work on it a *lot*."

"You work on it? How do you work on it?" I ask, imagination spinning off in all directions. And most of them look like my favorite filthy movie:

Accidental weird sex with big dick.

"I do yoga, a lot of yoga, some might call it *excessive* amounts of yoga. I take a lot of soothing herbal remedies. And I recently started on an all-vegan diet, which is really wholesome and helpful and awful honestly it is just the *worst—never* be vegan unless nearly every delicious food there is contributes to your uncanny ability to spiral out of control," he says, and then I really have to restrict my mind in some way. Picturing him bending his body into interesting shapes is the last thing I need. I can only just cope with the way he says it—all in this rambling run that seems to have no real beginning or end. It defies the laws of grammar, the same way a lot of his little speeches do.

And I am definitely starting to respond to that in new and interesting ways.

"So you eat bacon and sprout fur all over your face, basically."

"That is not exactly the way I would put it."

"Then how would you put it?"

"More like: werewolves do not exist," he says in a way that suggests he thinks he has me. This line of questioning is over now. Plus the key he just tried has slid into the lock. Soon he will be free of this absurdity—but oh man does he underestimate me.

"So how come you have these handcuffs fit for restraining large beasts whenever there is a full moon, huh?" I ask.

Then rattle them, just for good measure.

I even look a little smug about my fantasyland logic.

And then he takes me out with this:

"The chances of me getting into that with you are zero."

Seriously, I think my hair sets on fire. I never for one second thought he might have a real and quite obviously shameful reason for having them here, despite that being utterly obvious. There was all that weird *wanting* business that happened before, and the eye contact that followed. This must be like some *sex* thing, of the sort I have to know about immediately. The only problem is: he just explicitly stated that he will never answer.

So I have to attack from another angle, again.

"So you used them to hold your seventh victim down here."

"Man you are good at that."

"Good at what?"

"Getting information out of people."

"I thought we were just talking."

"I want to be just talking. Actually no—I want to be just undoing these handcuffs that I own for perfectly normal, legal reasons that have nothing to do with being a serial killer or a secret werewolf I swear to God. Now hold still so I can do this faster," he says, but how can I with that refusal ringing in my head? Just the absence of sex information is making me wriggle around. I bounce so much at one point that he starts to move too.

He has to pause and eye me—though of course that only makes it worse. Now I seem to be squirming and wriggling, and especially when I consider that he *still* hasn't unlocked it.

You know. Like he might not want to just yet.

"It seems to be taking a long time."

"I know; that's worrying me too."

"I'm not exactly worried."

"That is the part causing me the most stress."

"I thought it was my uncanny ability to make you spill your guts."

"All of it is bad, very bad, including the fact that these seem to be rusted shut."

"So you last used them a long time ago, huh?" I ask, but he is wise to my tactics now.

"The question you should be asking is: *oh my God, am I stuck here because he forgot to oil them?* Swiftly followed by: *this guy is the* worst."

"If you knew what my life was like, you wouldn't wonder why I was so disinterested in going back to it," I say, though I really don't think I mean to. I hardly even know I feel that way until it pops out. After all, my life is hardly full of hardship now. I go to college. I have friends. I went on a date only last week. Sometimes my mom calls from somewhere far away to ask me for money.

It really is not as bad as it was.

Though even he knows the badness is there.

He can probably smell it with his werewolf senses.

"I think I can guess, considering how unfazed you are by a kidnapping."

"I promise you I have never been kidnapped before in my whole life."

"But you probably do have some high, weird threshold for what constitutes exciting."

"What, so you think I'm some thrill seeker?" I ask, half laughing.

Until he answers, that is. Then I stop.

"No, I think you have no idea what your own worth is."

In fact, I think everything stops. Silence descends like a monster from the deep, so big and dark I can well imagine it spreading to the outside too. People have probably halted in their tracks. The only sound is the birds singing, but even that will soon be smothered. It feels like an affront to speak in the face of it, but after ten excruciating seconds I have to. I have to know if he means what I think he does.

"What would you say my worth is?" I ask, voice so faint a breeze could blow it away.

Or maybe just a few more words from him.

"So high that you should have no reason to ask the guy who took you hostage for his opinion on it. So high that you keep being mad no matter what I do or say," he tells me, and I just fly off into the upper atmosphere. Has anyone ever said anything like that to me? I try to think, but my mom crying on my arm and thanking me for holding back her hair is all I can come up with. Maybe Marnie saying my upper-arm fat looks okay or Brett Faber telling me I was really an ugly girl but he wanted to date me anyway.

Nothing that clear and good and most of all: *obvious*.

He says it like the whole thing is obvious, and not even a big deal.

I need to tell him that somehow it *is* a big deal.

That he is a big deal, to me, for saying it.

"But you make it so easy not to be," I try, and for a second it works. He gets this look on his face like the one I probably have on mine—like someone reversed everything and suddenly we have to see it the other way around. He even sits back a little, like he needs some distance from whatever this is.

And then there is a sound like metal crying.

Metal cries, and suddenly he has half a key in his hand.

He snapped the key off in the lock, at the sound of me saying what *he* is worth.

"Still think it's easy not to be mad?" he asks, kind of like this is funny.

Only it isn't, anymore. Instead it feels like this:

"If you could see what your panic looked like, you would probably understand. You might even get it just for hearing yourself say the stuff you just did—I mean if you could be me and I could be you for a second. But then I guess that's kind of the problem, right?"

"You think the problem is that I don't know my panic is fascinating?"

"No, I think the problem is that we live our lives unable to see ourselves through someone else's eyes," I say, not meaning to seem so heartfelt about it. For a second I sound like something lost at the bottom of the ocean, so it feels like a relief when he steers everything back toward light and jokey and oh Christ are we flirting? It feels like we are.

Or at least like I might be.

He says normal things like, "So I'm guessing you don't see a hairy, angry ex-con who left it too late to get a locksmith." And then I respond with:

"You got the hairy part right. But maybe without the disgust in the tone."

And not just to give back to him what he gave to me. His hair is driving me kind of crazy. I just want to get lost in it, as though he somehow has an enchanted forest all over his head and face. And other places, apparently.

"There would be disgust if you saw my back. I have this stripe of thick hair right down the middle of—"

"Like a wolf. You mean like a wolf, a big sexy wolf."

"That…how do you turn pretend *back hair* around on me?"

"It was easy—you just walked right into it."

"I so did not—back hair is disgusting."

"Yeah, I know, right—almost as gross as your great big, strong hands and your amazing height and your broad, manly shoulders," I say, then really should feel embarrassed. I usually feel embarrassed if I let slip with a compliment for a guy twice as sexy as I am. Yet somehow, with him it seems different. It feels like I have space to talk the way I want to—which puts the rest of my life in some serious shade, considering the situation.

Apparently, I am more comfortable being myself while handcuffed with him than I am with anyone else while completely free.

But when he speaks again I can really see why.

"My hands are like beaten-up shoes. Have you really seen them? Check out what my little finger does when I hold them all together," he says, then does just that. I have no idea what he thinks he's proving, however, apart from the fact that he broke them once and now they don't bend the right way. Oh, and that I am probably going to have lusty dreams about those hands tonight—a fact that he seems completely unaware of.

"Yeah," he says. "Yeah, not so hot now, huh?"

And then I have to explain.

I *want* to explain. I want him to see.

"Probably even hotter, to be honest," I say, but that just seems to make things more complicated. Now not only am I having weird illicit feelings about him, I am also somehow the one sexually harassing someone here. I swear he blushes, even though he doesn't seem like the type to blush. He seems like the type to ask someone in the middle of an orgy to scooch over so he can sit down and read his paper.

Yet here he just wants to flee.

"Okay, I'm going upstairs to get a hacksaw."

"But we haven't talked about the height part yet."

"Let's not talk about the height part."

"Not even to ask how tall you are exactly?"

"Tall enough that it's a pain in the ass."

"Yeah, I figured you felt that way."

"Oh yeah? How did you go about that?" he asks, quite clearly ready to never believe me no matter what I say. Hell, I'm ready to not believe me. I'm not even sure why I made that claim until it comes out all freshly formed. Certainly I doubt I have anything to back it up—until that just sort of comes out of me too.

"Well, the way you winced when I said the word *height* was something of a giveaway. Then there's the way you hunch."

"I do not hunch."

"Sure you do. You even let your shoulders kind of drop, as though holding them right will make you look even more enormous than you already are. Which is accurate—because your shoulders look like a fireplace around the hearth of an angry giant—but also unnecessary. I mean, if you just do it because you want to be a mild-mannered bookstore owner, the tweed and corduroy kind of accomplish that."

"Okay, *Columbo*."

"Did you just call me *Columbo*?"

"You just nailed me in about eight different ways. I think *Columbo* is apt. Also can we just pretend I did not say *nailed* there? I would really appreciate that," he says, but how can I possibly obey?

I get a frisson just from the way the word *sounds*.

I get a buzz from the accompanying hand gestures.

"I think I might have to disappoint you there."

"No, come on. This is not a fair conversation—and not just because you are obviously as sharp as the razor I have to use on my back hair. Be honest with me. You're some kind of psych major right?"

"I took one class. *One*. And besides, you're the guy who said that about worth."

"I got it from *Chicken Soup for the Soul*."

"You have never read one word of those books in your life."

"Got me again, *Poirot*."

"So now I'm a short, fat Belgian."

"You are so far from that it—" he starts to say, but stops himself just as he gets to the good part. That was going to be the good part, right? I think so, because then he holds up his hands as though my non-Belgian-ness is a thing he needs to back away from before he does something nuts.

Like roam his hands through the forests of my hair.

I think he might want to roam his hands through the forests of my hair. Why else would he stand up so abruptly? Or tell me that he is seriously going to get that hacksaw now? It could still be his terror of accidental kidnapping, or a genuine desire to set me free. But underneath I feel sure I can make out something else. It lies just below the surface of his gaze and eats at me every time our eyes meet.

Which is often. Our eyes are meeting now, even though he is currently backing toward the door. Hell, I think they keep meeting after he has dashed up the stairs. All I can see in my head is how dark they got just before he darted away. All I can feel is the pressure of them, stroking over every inch of skin that he allowed himself to look at. Nothing below the neck and never lingering on any of the overtly sexual parts of my face, but still somehow intense to me.

In fact, I think his restraint might have made it more so.

Like someone hovering a hand over an aching part of my body, but always refusing to touch. There was a tension to it that I can't deny, and wouldn't want to even if I could. It makes my body hum just thinking about it. I find myself testing the strength of the stuff that attaches me to the bed frame, to see just how long I might have left. Is it minutes? Or hours? The cuffs themselves are quite delicate looking so would probably take no more than sixty seconds. But the chain that is looped between the bed frame and the cuff, on the other hand…

That chain looks like it was last worn by Jacob Marley. Each link is the size of my fist. He could spend all week on that thing and still not get through it—but the problem is, why would he? He has no reason to choose that over the cuffs or the bed frame. I have to persuade him somehow, I think, then want to get Freud on fucking speed dial immediately.

What the hell is happening to me?

Why am I considering a thing like that?

Normal people do not consider things like that. But then, normal people do not light up inside when their jailer comes back down the stairs. They do not think *oh my God, he really is absolutely fucking gorgeous.*

Because he isn't, in truth. He looks nothing like the kind of guy Marnie goes for. He looks nothing like the kind of guy *I* go for—or so I thought. But now I know the real reason my type never really turned me on all that much. What I really want is this. What I really need is *this*. And that's why I draw the chain taut for him. Not the flimsy cuffs, or the battered bed frame. The chain that will take him until the end of time.

"Go ahead," I say to him, fully expecting him to say no.

Then he just sets to work wordlessly, and my whole world turns upside down.

Chapter Three

THE THING IS, I think he genuinely wants to saw through the chain and set me free. He works at it superhard, he really does. After half an hour of silently going at it, he has to sit back on his heels and take a breather. He even rips his glasses off in frustration and pinches the bridge of his nose. But still, deep down he had to be aware that he could have just hacked through the cuffs or the bed frame.

He would probably be done by now—if he really wanted to be.

But considering the electric spark of our current conversation, who would? Certainly not me. I could keep talking like this until the end of time. He just told me that his favorite book in the store is a rare edition of *Grimms' Fairy Tales* where the wolf in *Red Riding Hood* has an erection, which is awesome for two reasons. The first is that he quite clearly loves the old gruesome versions of the stories with everyone getting their feet cut off and strangling themselves with hair. And the second is his awkwardness when he realizes he just said *erection* to me. He even tries to downplay it.

"I mean, not like a full-on...you know...with...all of that," he says, before it occurs to him that he is unable to even be vague about it. The whole thing is a minefield, and he just exploded half his own face. He has to go back to feverishly sawing at the chain, but I can tell it hardly helps. Unintentionally filthy things are still waiting around every corner, just waiting to spring on us when we least expect them. He thought he was just innocently talking to me about books—the safest subject there is.

Then *bam,* suddenly we have a rampant cock right in the middle of it.

And when I tell him that I really love the sound of that, well. That obviously has a double meaning too. The only difference is that I, of course, totally 100 percent mean my double meaning. In fact, I come close to just shoving the real word in there instead of leaving it at *that.* Why bother being coy? I should have just gone with *I love dick* and been done with it.

A fact that I think he suspects. When he flicks that black-as-pitch gaze up at me, he also tilts his head to one side, as though to say *seriously*? As though to say *give me a goddamn break.* And I want to, I do. But somehow him needing that break seems to churn me up even more. I can feel it flaring inside me every time he tries to haul things back to something like sanity. He puts the brakes on.

Then I just go ahead and cut the line.

I throw ice all over the road.

I jam my foot down on the gas.

"Maybe you could show me later."

"I honestly have no idea whether to laugh at your chutzpah or just kill myself. Yeah, sure, I can show you the book later. The book. You can see the book once you are completely free and not having this conversation with me," he says, then clearly seems to think that puts an end to the matter. He even nods in this satisfied sort of way and puts the saw back to that chain.

But he is in for a surprise.

"Is the book in your pants?"

"You do not want what is in my pants, man."

"That enormous and terrifying, huh?" I say, and now it's my turn to be surprised. I expect him not to answer— or at least go with some kind of dismissal.

A wave of the hand, I think.

And instead get *this*.

"*Yes.* Yes. Oh, you thought I was exaggerating for effect? Ha ha ha *no.* Now can I just do this without talking about my gigantic penis, please?" he says, in a manner I think he intends as amusing. Hell, it is amusing, in all kinds of different ways. His delivery is electric all on its own. He emphasizes all the right words and pauses in all the right places, and when he is done I sort of adore him for it.

Plus there are the words themselves, which are hilarious.

Or would be if they were not about his huge dick.

Did he just say he has a huge dick? I think he did, but thinking does me no good in this particular situation.

Now my mind is flooded with some seriously graphic images, and all of them are doing stuff to my body and my face. I think an invisible hand grabs me between my legs. I know my mouth falls open.

And I say things kind of on autopilot.

"I probably would have been able to before."

"Before what, for the love of God?" he asks.

But I think he knows. He seems madder at himself than me.

And even more so after I answer.

"Before you said it was gigantic."

"Okay, so then if I say, 'Actually, I have a tiny one,' can we go back to just attempting to free you before somewhere around midnight?" he asks, which just makes me wonder.

What time is it exactly? It felt early before, but now it feels late.

Not that this bothers me in the least when he might be this close to cracking.

"But I know that you're lying."

"Maybe I was lying before. Maybe I just have a complex about it and want girls I capture to be superintimidated by the thought of my monster cock, when really I have two peas and a baby carrot," he says, but if he wants me to calm down he should really avoid words like *monster* or *cock* or even *baby carrot*.

It only makes me thirstier.

"That would probably sound believable if you had said it in a bragging way, were five foot four with hands like spiders, and did not seem so unwilling to be a tough guy in every single way. Your cardigan alone screams *my dick is bigger than your arm*."

"Well, not…not your whole arm…but…maybe from the elbow to the wrist…"

"Oh my God, oh my God, are you describing it to me?" I ask, though I really have no need to. I can see that this is literally what he's doing. He just seems to forget himself for a second, and kind of measures with his hands in the air. He even sizes up the limb in question, with his head on one side. It is simultaneously the most absurd and most arousing thing I've ever seen.

And that definitely shows in my voice.

It might even show on my face, too, because when he snaps his gaze back to me, he seems to realize what he's doing. He suddenly looks at his measuring hands as though they belong to someone else, then once he's established that no, they are indeed his, he definitely did that, he jumps up. He backs away, shaking his head, and finally he babbles. Oh God, the way he babbles.

"I have no idea I don't know what's happening to me I need to go lie down somewhere I need yoga lots of yoga this is all just too much. I feel hot inside my clothes I feel like I need to tear something off," he says, in a way clearly intended to make things better, while actually only making things way worse.

All he has to do is say *tearing* and *clothes*, followed by actually tearing them.

He yanks at one sleeve of his cardigan and I think I almost lose my mind.

"You have my full consent to do that," I say.

But of course that only backs him further into the corner.

A really, really awesome corner.

"You can't consent you are chained against your will to my bed do you understand that? I need permission, man. I need *yes yes yes* wholehearted yeses."

"To do what, oh my God, to do what?"

"Wow—so not getting into that with you."

"You might as well now you said it."

"I did not mean to say it. It just keeps coming out of me."

"So why not let a little more out?" I ask, but as soon as I do, I know I pushed too hard.

I seem too excited and greedy. He has to hold up both hands to ward me off.

"That right there is exactly how I get into terrible situations. I just allow myself a little more freedom and then suddenly there are naked women everywhere and lots of crazy stuff going on and I am doing a lot of things that make me very uncomfortable in the light of day."

"Stuff where people did not say yes?" I ask, though I will be honest.

I don't for one second think that's the answer.

I just know it will make him explain more—and it does.

"Christ, *no*. No. No. I would never force anyone to do anything. I just tend to feel sort of gross about…liking it so much. And especially now in front of a person who I have tied up in a very similar manner to possible other people who wanted me to do certain things while they were…in that state."

Certain things, I think. *In that state*, I think.

Then have to sit there calmly while my mind runs riot.

"So like spanking and bondage and felching and things."

"Do you even know what felching is or did you just throw that one in there with gleeful abandon?"

"A little from column A and a little from column B. Mostly from column B."

"And therefore quite obviously I should not be talking about this with you."

"Hey man—I watch porn. I know most stuff," I say, but am aware of how limited it sounds as soon as I do. I could be a teenage boy trying to impress my big brother, and his expression bears that out.

As does his response.

"That answer is not helping me at all. None of this is helping me at all. I just want to cut the chain and get you out of here so I can go back to my upstanding, decent, calm life," he says, so I try to go one better.

"I bet you could still be upstanding after you pinned me down and—" I start, but oh God, that is somehow way worse than all the other stuff. He actually puts his hands over his ears. He says *la la la* really loudly until I stop talking altogether, and even after I do he still seems like a ball of frustration and fury. "I am breaking this chain *now*; hold still," he says, then goes at it like a man possessed.

Possibly by the demons my potty mouth just set free.

Sadly for him, however, they are not so easily destroyed.

"If it would be any easier on you, we could just make out with a lot of tongue."

"Unsurprisingly, no, that would not be easier on me at all."

"Maybe you just don't find me attractive, then."

"Oh that ploy is so beneath you."

"But I was kind of serious this time."

"Okay I know there is still a possibility that you are just goading me into this, but on the off chance that you are really starting to wonder, I simply have to say. Honey, you are just about the most attractive woman I've ever had the misfortune of meeting. Not just in terms of your face—which, as awkward as it makes me feel to admit this is absolutely stunning, I mean those big amber eyes and the dimples and the apple cheeks and oh my God you look like a milk maid who wandered down from the Alps—but the way you *are*. Honestly the way you talk damn near makes my hair stand on end. For the last hour my heart has been pounding in my teeth. I think I may have blacked out briefly when you said that about being pinned," he says, and then I just cannot help myself. Whether I meant to get his real opinion or not, once I have it he needs to know.

I don't even care about how breathless I sound when I tell him.

"I think that might be the most amazing thing anyone has ever said to me."

"Honestly, that is pretty much the bare minimum of what you deserve."

"Or maybe *that* is the most amazing thing anyone has ever said to me."

"People should be saying this to you all the time. I just said it despite really not wanting to. It's simply a fact like water is wet and Nicholas Sparks writes derivative stilted nonsense."

"I can assure you no one has told me any of that before."

"Not even the stuff about the way you talk?"

"Most people call it *annoying*."

"It *is* annoying," he says, and for a second I actually feel a little disappointed. I was starting to think he really might be that one—you know the guy you read about in romance novels who just gets you and sees you want a spanking before you know you do—and it's kind of a let-down to think he might not be. Then twice as awesome when he adds: "But it's also fucking electrifying, man. *Too* electrifying. Wanting-to-do-stupidly-crazy-things electrifying."

"Can the stupidly crazy things be you kissing me now?" I ask, and don't even care about how desperate I sound. Why should I when he seems just as desperate? His eyes actually roll closed for a second. He has to make violent sweeping gestures with his hands.

And when he speaks, it feels more like he's telling himself than me.

"No. No. This chain is coming off," he says, then sets to it again with even more vigor than before. Not that it makes the blindest bit of difference.

"I don't think it's coming off."

"I know it's not coming off, but can we just pretend?"

"All right—oh hey, I think you made a dent in that one link!"

"You are an unbelievable nightmare sent from hell."

"But in a good way though, right? You just said in the good way."

"In the best possible way—*fuck*," he says, that last word so thick with frustration I almost feel sorry about it. In fact, if seeing him throw down the hacksaw and clench his fists was not so hot, I probably would. But as it is, I have room for only one emotion in my body right now, and that emotion is yes *I am* so *going to get the lay of my life any second*!

Though sadly, it seems I am *still* wrong about that.

"Okay, here is what we are going to do," he says, and I can just tell this is not going to be the answer I want. He does meditation breathing between each word. He just unfurled his big fists and his voice is perfectly measured. God, I never thought I'd want a guy to not be so measured. I roll my eyes at rowdy football players and hate bar fights. Everything here is the wrong way around—as evidenced by my reaction to his next words. "You are going to sleep in this bed, quietly, without asking any more questions about sex acts that you barely understand. Then in the morning I will go to the hardware store and get a pair of bolt cutters the size of a small building and just cut these suckers right off you. You will go back to your life and I will go back to mine and it will be like none of this ever happened," he says, and I just want to scream no, no, no.

At first, anyway.

But then it starts to dawn on me just what his little *keep calm and go to sleep idea* will really mean. It means I have to stay here, with him. All night, in the dark most likely. It means I get to talk more to him and persuade harder—not to mention other fun things. Oh my God, all of the other fun things. I bet he has no clue. He probably thinks this will be easy.

Oh bless him, he thinks it will be easy.

"That sounds like a great plan."

"I know it does."

"Really top-notch."

"Right?"

"Almost perfect in fact."

"Oh God, what?"

"I need the bathroom."

Chapter Four

THE GOOD NEWS is that the bathroom is right next to this little basement room. The bad news is that in order to get to it we have to heave the bed across the floor and jam it in the open door. And even then the whole thing is incredibly fraught. I have to sort of perch with one arm out like I'm reaching for help. I can hardly get my panties down, what with the chain that time forgot attached to my wrist.

Oh, and in the process of heaving, he sort of ends up on the wrong side of the door.

"No wait, wait, we have to start over; we did it wrong."

"We can't start over. I have to go now."

"At least let me climb out of here."

"Just turn your back."

"*Christ*, okay just wait a second, wait a second do not take any clothes off just yet. Give me a chance to blow my brains out first. I think I have a gun in here somewhere," he says, and though he quite clearly isn't serious—if only because there is nowhere in this austere room for a gun to be hiding—I kind of have to ask now. I mean, I feel like we should be making some headway by now.

And by headway I of course mean hot monkey love.

"Is it really that big a deal?"

"Having to stand over my captive while she pees? Yeah kind of a big deal. Usually comes with feelings of intense remorse and a lengthy prison sentence."

"Come on. You know that isn't going to happen."

"The remorse is already happening."

"Even though I don't mind one teeny tiny bit?"

"Well, considering you probably have Stockholm syndrome."

"I don't think Stockholm syndrome happens so fast. Or because your kidnapper has a supernice ass," I say, but I swear I do it only because he totally, totally does. The second he turns around it's pretty much all I can see. The corduroy hugs the curve of it like an overexcited hand, and when he moves I swear I can see muscles bunching there.

He has muscles in his butt.

Is it any wonder I feel the need to comment?

I doubt I could stop myself if he begged me—a point that proves true a second later.

"Please do not look at my ass while I attempt to not listen to your underwear coming off," he says, swiftly followed by me asking even more salacious things.

"Can you hear it sliding down my thighs?"

"No. All I can hear is the blood rushing in my ears."

"They are cotton with Tuesday on the bottom."

"Stop that. That is…not cool."

"Which one? Talk of my underwear or your backside?"

"Both of them. Both of them are not cool."

"But you *do* have a nice ass," I say, and when he sighs in response I think *okay, now you went too far*. Only to be surprised with the greatest answer to anything ever, in a voice as weary as worn stone.

"It's the Pilates."

Honestly, I think I might be in love with him.

"That why you have those arms too?"

"I can do handstand push-ups."

"Probably should not have said that."

"I know. As soon as it popped out, I thought: man that was a mistake."

Okay, now I *definitely* love him. At the very least I love how he can be both superstressed about something yet funny as fuck at the same time. Seriously, his laconicism is just beyond anything previously charted. It is beautiful and epic—they should mount it in the Louvre for people to marvel over. And though I imply that his arms are the reason I say what I say next…it's really that temperament of his that does it.

"Kind of want to throw these panties at you now."

"Please try to refrain. I really want to be a good guy here."

"You are being one, I promise. In fact you're being so good I kind of just want to make you be bad."

"Yeah, I'm getting that vibe. Or more accurately: that vibe is straddling my thighs while strangling me," he says, and it's like the chain instead of the cuffs all over again.

He can claim he wants out of this.

Yet still somehow he keeps making it worse.

"Is that what you like to do?" I ask, then have to hold my breath when he doesn't answer right away. It almost seems like he might really do it this time. Give me an answer filled to the gills with gory details. Tell me all about that time he went to a sex club and did some mutual strangling with a girl in a leather catsuit.

But sadly, I am mistaken.

Probably about all of it.

"Let's just get back in there. You done?"

"Yeah."

"Your panties back on?"

"Maybe."

"Put them back on and help me with this bed," he says, so I do.

But only because it presents other opportunities. It lets me stand next to him again, and take surreptitious peeks as we push. The first time we did this, I noticed his moustache is slightly darker than the lower part of his beard—or maybe slightly thicker, I think, once I get a second up-close look at it. And though all the hair kind of makes it seem like he has a mean mouth, he really doesn't.

In fact I think his upper lip is actually *plump*. Yeah, it looks a little plump to me, and even when his mouth is relaxed it kind of curves upward in this really—

"Your eyes are practically burning the side of my face."

"Then stop being so handsome."

"How can I when I never started?"

"Should I do a big speech now about how hot you are?"

"I would much rather you just help me push this bed," he says, and I obey.

But only because we keep almost touching when we do. His hand has to be real close to mine almost out of necessity, and any extrahard pushing tends to almost mash them together. At one point the bed suddenly screeches across the floor and both of us jerk forward, little fingers actually grazing before we can do anything to stop them.

I feel his skin. He feels my skin.

It makes him blush and sigh and me want more.

And I get it too. Halfway there, his leg rubs briefly against my leg. I think I feel the corduroy through my jeans—or at least it seems that way to me. My body is so primed I could probably make out a feather through a steel door. By the time the bed is back where it's supposed to be, I feel sort of enormous and far too hot. I might even be shaking, as ridiculous as that seems. I have to keep telling myself over and over that I met him a few hours ago and he chained me up in his basement.

But really I don't know what good I think that's going to do.

It barely puts a dent in whatever this is—and not just for me.

When he turns my way he seems the same way. His breath is coming hard and fast, and I somehow doubt it has anything to do with the exertion. I think it's something else. I think *this is it; this is where he's going to kiss me*. I can almost feel it. I know it; I am so certain I actually go up on tiptoe…

"I should probably get you something to sleep in."

God, I wish I had not gone up on tiptoe.

"Right. Sure. That would be great."

"I have some old pajamas."

"Sounds awesome," I say, unable to quite hide my disappointment.

Though it dissipates somewhat when he goes upstairs briefly and comes back with some. For a start they smell like him—so much so that I get a great wave of it while they're still folded. He offers them and suddenly my senses are full of cedar and old books and other stuff that should never make me swoon. If anything it reminds me of a trunk in an old lady's attic. One who practices witchcraft in her spare time.

And likes flannel a lot because oh my God they are flannel and they feel like butter and in a second I will feel them against my skin. All over my skin, rubbing in places they have probably rubbed him. Not only that, but once he hands them to me something else occurs in a delightful rush:

"How am I going to put them on?"

"Well you just…oh fuck," he says.

And there is my opening.

"I mean, you could help me…"

"That seems like a bad idea."

"No, no it's easy, honestly. You just need a pair of scissors and then you slowly, slowly ease the blades under the collar of my T-shirt and down my back," I say.

I honestly don't think I've ever had so much fun in my whole life.

"You want me to cut your clothes off. Is that what you're suggesting here? That I cut your top off your body and most probably your bra too—because I bet you don't want to sleep in that—and then maybe your jeans even though your jeans are not trapped by a pair of handcuffs in any way whatsoever."

"That sounds good to me."

"Okay fine, sure, why not."

"Really?"

"Absolutely. Turn around, I'll get right to it," he says, but the thing is I don't think he really expects me to. I think he's just moved from refusals to playing some kind of half-crazed game of chicken, and I know it for sure after I do what he asks. I turn and wait and wait, until finally I just have to ask if he's still there.

And he replies far too brightly.

"Just getting the scissors!" he says, as though I don't know what he's doing.

He expects me to flinch.

I will *never* flinch.

"Great."

"I'm going to make the first incision now."

"Awesome."

"You're not going to stop this, are you."

"You should have known I wouldn't," I say but honestly even I don't realize what this is going to be like. I think I imagine it to be vaguely exciting and kind of hard on him, instead of something that dissolves my spine. I feel the metal against my skin, and all the bone and cartilage just slide right out of my body. My legs lose the ability to hold me up—which makes sense as now there is nothing controlling them.

But other stuff comes as a shock.

Like the way my nipples stiffen when the scissors slide over my shoulder. My nipples actually stiffen over it, as though he's doing something sexual to me instead of the real fact of the matter: he just slowly, slowly snips through the material, one careful strand at a time. Though as the silence grows steadily thicker, I start to think that might be the problem. The slowness of it, and the way it sounds as each fiber parts. There is this wrenching quality to it that makes me think of skin being eased away from flesh.

He could cut me, I think.

Then almost drown in my own desire. I think of blood bright as berries and his mouth stained with a slick of it, and though I know that makes me wrong inside, good God being wrong feels so right. It feels like shedding that skin I just imagined. The T-shirt falls away and the new me is revealed underneath, as raw as a wound and so suddenly naked it sort of stings. I have to cover my bare breasts, but even that has a strange thrill to it.

And especially when I look over my shoulder at him.

I think of things like protecting my modesty, and go all weirdly weak—then even more so when I see his face. His eyes look lost at the bottom of an abandoned well. I think he might be trying to speak, but his mouth just moves around words that won't come out. But more than that: he takes a step forward. He raises his hand, like he might be about to do something to me. *Pull my hands away from my breasts*, I think.

Then I almost drop them, before he can.

Just so he can see that the answer is yes.

I have never wanted it to be yes more in my whole life. Not even after two years of dating Jimmy Henderson in high school, in a hotel room we paid for after prom. Not even after the hot dude at the Dairy Queen asked me out, and I spent the whole time in the movie theater just wanting him to put his hand up my skirt.

They were all perfect times to want to so much it makes my heart burst, but nothing matches this moment with a man I barely know. This beautiful, electric, beyond perfect moment that will surely end with the greatest words anyone has ever said to me.

Or you know. It could end like this:

"I need to…go…here…now."

Though honestly, I think it might be for the best.

Chapter Five

THINGS ARE DIFFERENT once I'm alone in the dark. I have time to think about everything from far away, instead of right up close and too claustrophobic to bear. I get some space from it; I can breathe without filling myself with it. Maybe it was all just a temporary madness, I think. I have leftover issues from a childhood spent with crazy people, and this is the result. Me lying naked beneath the covers of a strange man's bed—because of course it only occurs to me *now* that the pajamas cannot go on me any more than the clothes could come off. Rational thought has been restored, and that comes with consequences.

Like me cringing over how I behaved.

God, what made me behave like that? I probably freaked him out forever. I know I freaked myself out. I had no idea I had all of those feelings—though I can hardly blame myself for that. It's not like I've had a lot of opportunity to discover I enjoy being tied up and cut out of my clothes. Even just thinking about it makes me wonder what sort of person I am. Or what sort of person he must believe me to be.

Probably a huge pervert, I think, then want to super-glue my hands to my face.

And not just because of the embarrassment. There is also the fact that creeps up on me sometime just south of two in the morning: I really *like* him. I like everything about him. I've never liked everything about a guy before. In truth, now that I think about it, I don't think I've ever liked a guy. Those things I thought were crushes weren't anything close to it at all.

This is a crush.

This is what it feels like to want someone, to crave their company, to miss talking to them, even though you stopped only a couple of hours ago. I just want to do it all over again—but of course now I can never. I fucked it up with my forwardness. Next time we meet it will probably be a cordial handshake and nothing more, and the thought kind of rocks me to my core. I find my eyes actually stinging at the thought, and though that seems ridiculous I understand why.

It comes to me in a wave of realization:

I am lonely. I am lonely for someone like me. My real species left me behind on this rock, and I have spent my whole life among strangers. I just didn't know it until now, and even then I only do because I drove the other one away. I fucked it up, the way I always fuck up every-thing. I did this and now the last remaining member of my race is probably upstairs in his apartment hating me.

Or so I think.

Until a voice suddenly rings out in the darkness.

"I just need to get my toothbrush."

I swear, I almost scream. The only thing that stops me before I can is the content of the words—so supremely ordinary and simple it would be insane to make a sound like that. And it would definitely be insane to cry with relief. I need to get a grip on myself, honestly. I have no idea what is wrong with me. He probably still hates me anyway and is just superworried about oral hygiene.

Only then…oh then he says this:

"Are you awake, Rosie? Rosie? I feel pretty sure that you are, considering there is no breathing going on. Which I am hoping means you're holding your breath. Unless you died, of course. Oh God, did you die? Please make a sign to show me you did not die. Doesn't have to be a big sign, if you're still mad at me for running out on you like that. Occurred to me afterward you probably couldn't put the pajamas on, so I've just been up there wondering about that. And by that I mean you struggling to stay warm, not you half hanging out of pajamas—Christ, you know what I mean. Do you?"

And when he's done, those tears I thought were stupid to cry leak out of my eyes. I feel them make two stripes over each cheek, cool and good and sweet.

He thinks I should be mad at him.

He worries that I am dead.

"Yes. Yes God yes I do yes."

"You okay, kid?" he asks, and though that last word reminds me of the chasm between us, the rest of it is amazing. *You okay*, he said—because he can hear the tears in my voice most likely. He hears and cares, and that makes me just about burst out with things I shouldn't tell him.

"Yeah. Now I am. The last surviving member of my species still likes me," I say, which seems as though it might be far too much. But the good part is: he doesn't make me pay for it.

"If that means me, of course I do. Of course I do. You didn't think me leaving meant I hated you, did you? I left because I wanted to keep cool. But you should probably know I came back because I—"

"You what? Please Lord please finish that sentence."

"I wanted to talk to you some more," he says, and I don't know what affects me more.

The words themselves or the fact he says them so simply.

Like they are obvious, and inescapable.

"I wish I could say how good that is to hear."

"I wouldn't mind you trying for me."

"As good as swimming in chocolate sandwiches."

"That does sound pretty amazing."

"As good as kisses at Christmas."

"Oh yeah, and like, in a room full of decorations."

"So many decorations they hurt your eyes."

"And a toy *Polar Express* goes round and round on a track."

"Do you have a *Polar Express*, Han?"

"I might."

"You're so sexy," I say, and only afterward think he might take it the wrong way. It sounds kind of like sarcasm even though I mean it more than anything. I mean it so much that I almost rush to add that I was being straight with him then, and only stop because he does something awesome.

He gets exactly what I was suggesting.

And he gives it back.

"You should see me playing with it."

"I am. I'm picturing it right now."

"I wear a conductor's hat and have a pipe."

"Oh my God oh my God a pipe that you smoke?" I ask, only this time I kind of want it to sound sarcastic. My excitement was ridiculous before. Now it's just plain weird.

"Yeah—mostly so I can pretend I gave up cigarettes," he says, but even that sounds cool to me. Now all I can see behind my eyes is him in some bar with that denim jacket on, hair probably wilder than it is here with a smoke jutting out from between those gorgeous lips.

"Who cares? I bet it smells amazing."

"Like an old stove in a cottage in England."

"You're killing me, I am dying, I am dead."

"Please don't be. I already panicked once tonight about that."

"Okay—I am totally alive, like really superalive."

"That sounds better. That sounds right," he says, and I almost go on with this flirting in the dark. I even know what I want to say next: *So right that we can kiss now?*

But I stop short when it occurs to me that he means something else.

And I'm dead-on—he means something lovely.

"You are so alive you hurt my eyes."

"I want to say that sounds terrible, but it doesn't," I say, though I know I do it too soft. I know he said that too soft. We sound like we want to marry each other immediately—which probably explains his response.

"Okay, well I should probably..."

"Go get your toothbrush?"

"Yeah. That," he says, but to his credit he sounds kind of sad about it. The flight of fantasy is over again, and now we're back to reality.

Hell, even I join in.

"Why is it even down here?"

"Well, this is usually where I brush my teeth. I mean on an ordinary day I don't do it using water from a vase of flowers on my counter in the store before sleeping between two bookshelves," he says, and at first I go to talk about some other nonsense, as though that concept means barely anything.

But then I realize.

"Wait—so you don't live in the apartment above the store?"

"No, of course not. Why would I have this down here if I did?"

"I have no fucking clue now that I think about it. I guess I just assumed that you lived somewhere other than a basement and this was like...your sex den."

"Nope, that is pretty much me. Sex den dweller."

"And you just...let me have it for the night."

"I think *let* is kind of a strong word."

"Not really. You could have slept down here too."

"That's a nice fantasy, Grandma."

"You could have! I would have slept on the floor."

"And I would have poked out my brain with a fork," he says, and though I cannot see even the slightest part of him in the pitch-black dark, I can picture his expression more clearly than I can remember the face of my own mother. One eyebrow will be up, and his will be halfway to the heavens, and his mouth will be quirked in that world-weary way that just about slays me.

It's slaying me now, and I can't even see it.

"I wouldn't have tried to have sex with you again."

"Is that what you were doing before?"

"Kind of. Maybe. Did I do it that badly?"

"More like much too well," he says.

After which I am very, very glad for that darkness. Now he has no idea that those words make me shiver. Or that my brain is now whirring a thousand miles a minute over the idea of what *too well* might mean. He could have gotten hard, I think, once all of my clothes were off. Or maybe something like that happened before then, when I went to kiss him.

I thought it was nothing at the time.

But in light of this revelation...maybe not.

"I almost wore your resistance down, huh?"

"I really don't want to say how close you came."

"I promise I won't try again."

"You swear it?"

"I swear."

"Just friends, okay?"

"I can do that."

"Good friends."

"Best friends."

"Beings from the same planet," he says, and then I almost break. I could just say to him: *Hey, how about after this we just go on a date?*

But I know why I don't.

"Night, Rosie," he says.

And after that there is only one answer.

"Night, Han."

Chapter Six

I TRY NOT to obsess about the whole thing too much. But the thing is, it's kind of hard not to when this reminder is still around my wrist. He cut the chain but not the cuff, and now that thin metal band is all I can think about. It clatters against my desk when I go to take notes in nineteenth-century literature, and slides against the skin so softly every time I lift my arm or lower my arm or do it all on purpose so I can feel it again.

And of course Marnie comments on it.

Where did you get the bracelet? she asks, as we fill our trays with cafeteria slop. I'm just reaching for more gelatinous goo number seven with a side of banana-something, and my sleeve comes up. The metal catches the light, so pretty for a second I can totally understand why she would think that. For a moment even I think the same. I try to remember where I bought such a nice piece of jewelry.

Swiftly followed by a sucker-punch of memory.

Not to mention the slap of having to come up with an explanation. So far, she hasn't asked me a single thing about any of this. She never wondered where I was or seemed curious as to how I got away. I just turned up to class like usual and she launched right into this tirade about Martin Dolarhyde and his refusal to call her when she needs him to, while I sat there in some kind of post-crush shock.

Or was it post-trauma shock?

It feels like both.

It feels like all of that.

How am I supposed to say anything to her when it's all of that? Suddenly the cuff around my wrist seems like a scarlet A. It makes my face heat and my body go all funny in ways I barely understand. I didn't do anything to be ashamed of. I'm not about to do anything to be ashamed of. He just wants to be friends anyway, so what does it even matter?

"Saw it in some junk store," I say.

Then tug my sweater down too quickly.

Though of course tugging my sweater down too quickly just makes me think of my clothes, still cut up somewhere on the floor of his basement. And the jacket he gave me to wear back to campus. The too-big leather that seemed somehow so small and snug once it was zipped up over my bare breasts. Every time I moved it felt like something cool and soft stroking something far too sensitive, though I did my best to keep it inside. *He just wants to be friends*, I think.

Do friends call each other after two days?

I never have with Marnie, but that hardly means anything. Some days I'm not even sure if we're really buddies at all. At best she seems to view me as a necessary evil, and at worst I am a vague irritation she wants to shake. My one real use to her is as a partner in one of her schemes, and though the last one turned out well I realize it should have gone way worse for me. I could have been killed.

So probably best not to judge by that standard.

I have to go by more normal rules of the sort other people have. I overhear Cassandra Yates talking about texting her bestie all the time, which makes it seem like it wouldn't be so bad. But then I wonder if *bestie* is overstating it, considering it was just one long night of mostly misunderstanding each other and me throwing myself at him. Playing it supercool seems like the best option, in light of that.

But sadly for me, I am so bad at it.

I was bad at it right in front of him, and I'm worse at it now. Marnie has finished her meal and I'm still chewing the first bite, my mind so firmly on other things that I forget to swallow. I walk to my next class thinking of his face when I turned around, and lose almost all of a lecture to the words he said in the dark. *You are so alive*, he said, even though everyone else in the world seems to think I'm recently deceased.

Maybe I am, with them.

But I wasn't with him.

I was someone else—someone I want to be again. I just have to approach the whole thing from the right angle, instead of one that makes him flip out. And then it occurs to me, in a blinding flash that probably accompanies all great ideas: I could take his jacket back. Of course, I could take his jacket back. That makes perfect sense. No one could think that was a bad thing, except for me once I'm standing outside his store.

I find myself doing crazy things, like taking two steps sideways in case he sees me through his window while I'm building up to whatever this is. I practice what to say over and over in my head, as though suddenly it won't be easy anymore. In fact, I think I fear that very thing: I will go in and all the magic I've built up in my head will melt away to reveal the bedrock of reality underneath.

It was just a fever dream.

It was nothing—and I'm going to prove it right now. I march up the door, intent on just being breezy and near indifferent. *Here you go*, I will say, and he will say thank you and we will proceed from there in a very cordial fashion. Nothing but 100 percent total friendliness, no question about it. We might even shake hands, I think, and then I get to the glass and realize that I am a total fucking idiot.

There is no way I can ever be his friend.

As soon as I see him framed beneath the closed sign tacked to the door, I get it. He is just standing about a foot from it, eyes so fixed on me that I know he saw me across the street. He saw and he waited for me to cross and now he no more understands what to do than I did yesterday or the day before. I can practically see everything warring on his face—caught between the fake hope that we could be pals and the knowledge that we are definitely not.

And I think the latter is winning.

For the longest moment in the world, he doesn't do anything. He just looks and looks in a way that says I should probably go—and in all honesty, I almost do. I come *this* close to walking away altogether, heartsick and sore from it but sure it's the right thing to do. It wasn't what I thought it was, after all. It was nothing, I think, and so I put my hand against the glass in good-bye.

Or at least, I pretend I put it there to say good-bye.

I pretend, but as soon as his gaze goes to it I know. He sees the bracelet still around my wrist—the one I could have had cut off or picked off or yanked off if I'm being honest but didn't—and it must seem obvious. It feels obvious, all the way down to my bones. They practically vibrate when he looks back at me, half-weary and all-accepting and so goddamn gorgeous.

And then he walks to the door as though through a dream, and I am *done*. Everything is all over for me. I will never recover from the way he does that, so slow it feels exciting but so inexorable I can think only one thing. He cannot help it. He could no more help it than I could coming here. We've infected each other somehow, and the disease is deadly.

It forces him to unlock the door, one agonizing bolt at a time. Eyes always on me, in a way that wrings me out and washes me away. I swear in all my days no one has ever looked at me the way he does. He looks hungry, I think. He looks compelled by strange, new forces beyond his control.

But I understand how that feels, when he finally opens the door.

I do not mean to launch myself at him, as though my feet have wings.

I do not mean to jump into his arms, and kiss him hard enough to kill.

And yet that is exactly what I do, almost against my will.

As soon as I start, I sort of want to stop. However, there are two problems with doing so. The first is that his mouth is fucking amazing and detaching myself from it is harder than cutting through a three-inch-thick chain. And the second is so unexpected it sort of gets me in the gut.

He seems to feel the same.

No, not even *seems*. He *definitely* does. I can sense some tiny part of him trying to pull away, just as there is some tiny part of me. He tries kind of leaning to the right a little, and his hands go to my waist. It's just that they don't go to my waist to push me away. They go to my waist to hold me there. And that twisting and turning he's doing? It only really draws him in deeper. He ends up almost curled over me, as big as a house and twice as brilliant because of it, arms almost in a bear hug around me.

I swear I could live there.

I could just roll myself up in his suddenly dissolving restraint, and for a moment I do. I revel in it. I wrap my arms around him right back, mouth so greedy I feel as though I'm eating him. At one point I think I actually bite his lip, but I have no regrets. How can I when he tastes this good? He said he smoked a pipe, but I thought smoking a pipe would probably translate into ugly old tobacco breath. Not a bonfire of burnt caramel in the middle of an ancient wood. Not this thing that makes me so crazy.

And then there's his beard oh my God his beard. How come I can't stand stubble but a full-on face garden feels like this? It burns, but in the best possible fucking way. My face is going to look like I stained it eating strawberry jam, but I don't care. I just want to keep doing this and doing this until we absolutely have to stop. Maybe for bathroom breaks—and possibly not even then.

I'm not even sure if a sudden meteorite strike could do it. Even when he pulls away briefly for air, he can't seem to break contact completely. He has to keep shoving his hands into my hair in the weirdest, fiercest possible way—until all of it is pretty much standing on end. And when he looks at me oh when he looks at me his eyes are as dazed and feverish as my own.

He looks like he can't ever get enough.

Not even when we're standing a hairsbreadth apart.

Not even when we just stopped kissing seven seconds ago.

"I have to…I have to…I have to…" he says, but doesn't seem to know how to end the sentence. I think most of him wants to say *take a second* or maybe *stop*, but at least some is just dying to tell me the very thing on my own lips. *Get closer*, I think.

Then realize I didn't just think it at all.

I said it aloud, like some lust-crazed maniac.

But the best part is: he agrees. He actually agrees with me. "Yeah that too, God help me that too," he says, and then for one glorious second seems to lean in like he wants to taste my lips again. Like he can hardly stand not to. I think it takes almost everything he has to take a step back, and even after he has to clench his fists to stop them going back to my hair.

Or my waist.

Or my other things.

Oh man, I think he wants to touch my other things.

"Let me just calm down for a second okay?" he tries.

Though he has to know the battle is already lost.

"That's sort of like asking a fellow starving man to help you stop eating."

"At least stay where you are. Just stay where you are and try not to—"

"Try not to what?"

"Wriggle around so much."

"I didn't realize I was."

"You aren't; it just feels like you are," he says, so despairingly I sort of want to do as he asks. Be still and be calm and not bother him. But then I remember what really stands in our way now: absolutely nothing. I'm not his captive anymore. I can leave anytime I want to, and choose to do whatever I please. There are no chains on me anymore—or at least not literally.

Figuratively, on the other hand…

Oh figuratively I can feel the metal around my wrist like a brand.

"Maybe we can just sit down for second," he says, but still it burns.

It makes me agitated and bullish when I want to be anything but.

"Why do you want to sit down?"

"Oh I don't know. So we can share stories, talk about old times, learn little details about each other the way people usually do before they turn into angry bears in heat."

"So that's why you're against this. You want to get to know each other before we have all the sex."

"Well no, not exactly. I was thinking more that we could talk and *never* have the sex."

"I'm not sure I can agree to never having the sex."

"Oh come on, it'll be easy. It should be easy anyway."

"Why—because I'm no longer your captive?"

"No because I'm a hundred years old. Girls like you should not want to date guys who are a hundred years old. Guys that are a hundred years old are creepy for wanting to date girls like you. I feel creepy right now," he says, but I can sense that's not the whole of it. It can't possibly be, considering what I can now see pretty clearly in the dying but still bright light from outside.

"Just be honest. You're thirty-two right?" I ask, half sure he will still try to deny it. I think he actually tried to claim he was forty-something the other night, and believe he will try to stick to that.

So when he doesn't it's a joy and a pleasure.

"I'm thirty-one, but that's still too much."

"Seven years is too much?"

"It feels like too much. My criminal record feels like too much. That bracelet on your wrist is definitely, one hundred percent too much," he says, and quite obviously thinks he has me there. He honestly has no idea that I have him.

"You called it a bracelet," I say, and can hardly keep the teasing triumph from my voice. Much to his irritation. He throws up his hands when he realizes—and in such a cool way. There's all this regret in it, no doubt about that. But there's a kind of happiness too. I can see him smiling around his frustration. I can hear it singing in his voice.

"Of course I did. I see what this is, okay? I get it."

"You get that I want you to tie me up?"

"Don't say 'tie me up.'"

"And hold me down."

"Or that one, don't say that one either," he says, but when he does it he wags his finger at me. He actually *wags* it. Oh, it thrills me to my core. It makes me think of all the other things he could do, to show me what a bad girl I am.

"And punish me."

"Are you kidding me you're getting worse! This is a nightmare this is an absolute nightmare," he says, then seems to need a second to gather himself before he can go on. Even that is sexy, however. The way he runs a steadying hand through all that hair—and oh God, the tamer things he then says. "Okay, look, Rosie. I can maybe consider *possibly* having some sort of very affectionate courtship with you. There is room for tea drinking and hand-holding and maybe a little light, heavy petting at the back of a movie theater playing something French. But anything beyond that is just out of bounds."

I mean, did he just say *French movie*?

He wants to *court* me?

He has to know he's only making me wilder.

"Why does it have to be out of bounds?"

"Because I don't like myself when I behave that way, honey. I don't enjoy doing those things."

"There's nothing wrong with enjoying a little light bondage."

"Yeah, but there is something wrong with enjoying some girl you caught vandalizing your store being chained up in your basement. There is something wrong with wanting to—" he starts, but yet again he cuts himself off before he can get to the good part. The part I crave so much that I don't really care about the firm shake of his head or the way he puts his hands on his hips.

Like he means business, I think.

But I don't give a damn.

"Wanting to what?"

"Seriously, do you have to sound breathless when you say that? You could at least try to be casual about it. Throw in a shrug of your shoulder. Not look at me so intently."

"If I do that will you entertain the notion? Because I can, you know. I can look at you in a completely nonserious way if you need me to. We can make all of this as light and fun as you like."

"Okay, as much as I like the idea of light and fun, I can't fully imagine how that would go, considering my proclivities," he says, leaving me even more greedy for information than I was before. The very word has me hanging on the edge of some overexcited precipice, so sure that he's going to hold back again that I almost reel myself in. I get a grip on myself, just as he finishes with this: "I tend to get intense. And rough."

And yeah, I know I shouldn't get so giddy over *rough*. *Intense*, maybe sure okay.

But *rough* could mean all manner of horrible things. It could mean new bracelets on my wrists made of bruises and a fistful of my hair as he fucks me. He could *fuck* me, I think.

Then to my dismay my body just goes *insane*.

I think someone uncorks a champagne bottle inside me, after an angry giant shook it for a thousand years. Every part of me is fizzing, to the point where I no longer have control over myself. I'm practically jigging on the spot. My hair feels like it's standing on end—and worse things, oh so many worse things. I know for a start that my nipples are straining through my T-shirt. I almost wish I hadn't worn one, it looks so bad.

But at the same time I'm glad I did.

I'm glad glad glad—and doubly so over my equally disobedient mouth. Part of me wants to hold back a little. He seems so worried about all of this that it feels a little wrong to push. As though *I* am really the aggressor, and he's my innocent victim. And yet another part of me, this fizzing shaking wild let-loose part, just does not give a flying fuck.

I practically curl my tongue around my next words.

"They don't have to be mutually exclusive."

"I just told you I kind of enjoyed tying you up in my basement. That doesn't seem, oh I don't know, a touch dark to you? Just a little bit on the wrong side of terrifying?"

"It probably would have been if you'd acted on it. If you had done something against my will or at any point seemed as though you thought that was a good and viable option. But the fact that you found the idea itself disgusting says to me what should be pretty obvious to you: that there's a huge difference between what we want in our fantasies and what we do in real life," I say, but here's the thing:

He doesn't seem to think that's obvious at all.

In fact, he looks so stunned by this revelation that I have to wonder how he functioned before. I mean what did he think? That having a kink for bondage was corrupting his immortal soul? He must have, because after a second he adds "There has to be a line." As though he doesn't make one all the time. As though he fails to police them, when really he polices them so regularly and with such care I have to be the one who pushes him into the slightest thing.

But boy, am I happy to do it.

"So draw it then. You tell me where I shouldn't cross and I'll stay on the other side."

"You think *you're* the one who has to stay on the other side?"

"I'm not the one backing away," I say, and he looks stunned for the second time in as many minutes. He has to stop the incessant pacing just to process this—though he replaces it quickly with a lot of clenching and unclenching of his fists. And some thinking of such an intense type that it actually shows on his face. I can almost see his eyes darting back-and-forth like he's trying to solve a math problem. His frown is three fathoms deep, and I don't think it's out of anger.

I think it's out of nervousness or worry. When it finally breaks, even *I* feel relieved—and not just because it was making me antsy just looking at him hash it out with himself.

Some of it is definitely the giving in.

Oh the giving in.

"All right. All right. Let's say I set boundaries and limits."

"What sort of boundaries and limits?" I say, imagining chastity belts.

And sadly I am not far off.

"Well, for a start, no full sex."

"Oh come *on*, that—"

"No, no, I mean it. You want to do this? We do it my way," he says, and despite the slight sting of disappointment, I have to be honest. I sort of enjoy him talking that way. I like how grave his voice goes. I love how he draws a line with one big hand.

Though of course I see no reason to let on.

"Okay. But I have to say your way sounds super not-fun."

"You got that right. Think of this more like BDSM school," he says in a way that suggests he honestly thinks this will be the final boring nail in the coffin. He cannot possibly know that my head is already full of the potential syllabus for such a place. Or that said syllabus is not even the most exciting thing.

The fact that he said *BDSM* is. He said it aloud just like that, as though it's a real thing that actual people do. It's not just for show in porn or pretend in books, or only allowed in nightclubs with everyone wearing leather and red lipstick. It's just something you can talk about and make and have.

I can have this, if I really want it.

"Sounding a little more fun now."

"No, no. This is not fun. This is serious, with safe words. Safe words and long conversations about what we can and can't do at all times."

"I can do anything you want," I say, and just for a second wonder if I might live to regret that offer. I just sound so breathless about it, and give so much of myself in it. He could really do some awful things to me, if he were so inclined. He could say that he wants to cut me, and I might let him try.

But then I remember whom I'm dealing with.

"You don't even know what you're getting into. What if I suddenly decide I want to shave all your body hair off with a straight razor?"

I mean, honestly.

Does he think that sounds *bad*? I think I go weak all over just at the idea of it—despite the fact that the idea is shrouded in mystery to me. I see him kneeling between my legs with something Sweeney Todd might use, those burning bright eyes on my face the whole time, but beyond that I just don't know. I can't quite picture someone doing it.

But man I have fun trying.

"Are you serious? That sounds incredible."

"Okay so that was a bad example. How about if I blindfold you and make you feel your way around harrowing obstacles until you find various parts of my naked body?"

"Oh my *God*."

"And that excites you too…all right. Is there anything that doesn't?" he asks, and though he packs a lot of incredulity into that one little sentence I can tell he really means it. He's really asking me where *my* limits are, in a way that seems light and sexy no matter what he claims about serious sex.

At the very least, it feels pretty easy to say.

"I'm kind of nervous about gang bangs."

Though once I have, I realize my mistake. I let myself forget that he is probably expecting something tame. That he hopes for something tame, so as to not die of a fucking embolism.

"That…that…is never…I would never…I am speechless right now," he says, which is bad enough on its own. But then there is the way he looks as he does it: all big eyes and open mouth. You could put him under *taken aback* in the dictionary. He even sways away from me, like the very embodiment of *whoa*. Clearly, gang bangs were never going to be on the menu.

And now I have to squirm over the fact that I ever thought they were.

"If it helps, you could pretend I didn't say that."

"Yes please that would be awesome."

"Not your kind of thing huh?"

"Not even slightly, not even a little bit. I mean aside from the horror of the whole idea—which is extensive, believe me—I also tend to be a little more…"

"More…?" I ask, pressing for what I feel sure will be the word *prudish*.

And then he hits me with *this*.

"Possessive."

"Oh man."

"That shouldn't be a good thing to you."

"Even though you mean it in the sexy way."

"You don't know that. I could be mean and jealous and make you wear sacks out in public in case men look at your boobs," he says, then waits for an appalled reaction that will never come. Instead, I burst into giggles. And I do it so well that after a second he has to concede. "I know, I couldn't even say that with a straight face. I guess what I like in bed really *is* different to how I am in reality."

"You're honestly only just realizing that?"

"I don't think real hard about what I like in bed. I just tend to cordon it off in a section of my mind labelled *under no circumstances*."

"And now it's time to let that part out to play."

"Out to play? Seriously?" he asks, and though I know he's mocking me I don't care.

Because his mocking is so incredibly awesome. He must have a degree in incredulity, I swear to God. Even his head tilt is so masterfully done I want to just applaud for a second. In fact, the only reason I don't is that the need to get things going is now so strong I can feel it in my teeth. My fillings are practically starting to shake out.

And it makes me say some pretty dubious things.

"Yeah, absolutely. We just make it all a game. You are the angry bookstore owner and I am the bad girl."

"Oh, I don't know about that. It seems pretty close to the bone."

"Then say your safe word: *werewolf*."

"I get a safe word too?"

"Sure you do. You feel like fantasy and reality are colliding, you just tell me to stop."

"I feel like fantasy and reality are colliding please stop," he says, in so deadpan a way I could almost believe he meant it. If it were not for the thing we just discussed.

And that he hasn't used.

"Safe word, Han."

"Goddammit," he says, because that's the other fun thing about safe words—apart from the friendly little net they provide. They make you tell the truth almost against your will. He looks genuinely angry that his *no* has been exposed as the sham it is, from the clenched fist to his newly wrestling eyebrows.

But that just makes it all the more fun to go through with this. It makes it more real, when I reach out just ever so slightly and tilt a book out of its place on the shelf.

Then let it fall.

"Oops," I say.

And to my delight he knows exactly what I mean.

"Oh, not the books."

"I know, so bad, right?" I tell him.

Before moving on to the next one.

"Please no, that one's a hundred years old."

"And I just touched it with my filthy fingers."

"Why you gotta be this way?"

"I can be worse if you want."

"You wouldn't," he says in such a wary, warning sort of tone that I fail to see how I can do anything else. His gleaming black eyes practically guarantee it. Next thing I know the hundred-year-old book is in my hands and then uh-oh I wonder what has to happen now?

"I bet this book tastes so good."

"Don't you dare."

"Oh I can't wait to just lick…"

"Okay that's enough," he says, but if he really meant it he would tell me, right? He would use that word and I would put the book back on the shelf and we need never speak about it again. And when that doesn't happen—not even after I curl my tongue so close to the spine I feel sure I can taste dust—I have to imagine he wants me to carry on. Hell, his threshold appears to be higher than mine.

I don't want to lick this lovely edition of *Great Expectations*.

But I will do it, in the name of hot sex.

I will get closer and closer until the only thing he can see are my eyes over the top of the book and all I can feel is the tension between us and then just as I'm really going to have to break, he breaks first. Thank God, he breaks first.

Or maybe *thank God* is not quite the right way to put it. Not when I feel those big hands right on my hips, so sudden and forceful I somehow drop the book. Honest to God I do, even though I could swear I was holding it so tightly I almost made out the print inside with my fingertips. My hands are still sweaty from the death grip, and yet still here we are.

And just in case that wasn't bad enough:

I let out this little noise. This little frightened noise that immediately puts him back on edge. That fierce light leaves his eyes and I feel him go to draw back—until I get a handle on things again. I remember what this is and what I want, and I let him know in no uncertain terms. "Take your filthy hands off me," I sneer at him, and this time he keeps on course. He understands.

Oh man does he ever understand. He all but drags me around, in this one rough move that shoves my heart into my throat. I'm sort of glad it does, however. The very last thing I want is another startled sound coming out of me, and with a massive internal organ in the way the chance of that is slim. For a second all I can do is swallow and swallow and struggle to breathe, but that works out well for everyone.

It keeps me in this heightened state of *what the fuck is this going to be?*

And it lets him just carry right on beyond any point I thought he would. I mean, we are technically in the middle of his completely open-to-the-public store. Someone could walk down to this book-lined corner at any time. They might be in need of a copy of Kafka and instead come across two people doing some really dirty things.

Some really, *really* dirty things.

No honestly, I mean dirty. He does not start me off easy. I assume his hands are just straying to the tops of my thighs to test things out—so good and slow and strong that this in itself is an intensely sexual experience. His fingers are so long they almost circle me in places I should not be circled, and his grip is unbelievable. Like being cradled in the most pressurized sense possible. Like he's squeezing without squeezing me, I think.

Then just as I'm in the middle of that, he only goes and gets ahold of the hem of my skirt. And then he slowly, oh so slowly oh everything is so slowly, starts to *lift it*. Past my thighs and up to the underside of my ass and oh my God *beyond that*. He goes *over* my ass. Anyone who comes to the end of the row now will absolutely see my underwear-covered backside—an idea that almost makes me glance over my shoulder or say a word. In fact, the only thing that halts me in my tracks is the thought of the consequences.

The most incredible arousal of my life might stop. I could go back to the faint fluttering pulses I felt before, instead of this pounding, aching, melting sensation that is currently pouring through me. One of his fingers brushes the edges of the elastic and I just about go supernova. The insides of my thighs seem to thrum. My clit actually swells—you know the way it always does in filthy stories. It gets big, I think, and really sensitive, to the point where the slightest thing sends slippery tingles all the way through me.

Like when he starts to ease those panties down my legs—oh that sure does it. Though whether that move is a slight thing is debatable. It sort of seems more enormous than anything else, but even so the point still stands. I get that lovely rolling buzz usually reserved for far more sexual moments. A guy's face between my thighs usually pushes me to this point, or maybe more than that.

Yet I'm there already with Han.

I'm shaking with it, I think, in a way that makes it hard to keep standing. I sort of want to squat, and manage to avoid such an embarrassing thing only by bracing myself against the bookshelf. Just with one hand, and just on one shelf—so that he won't think so much of it—but still there all the same. And once I do it I can endure just about anything.

Except him lifting the skirt up over my bare bottom.

And then bending me at the goddamn waist.

Yeah after that I do not know what happens to me. I think I struggle, but somehow that only makes the whole thing more filthy and forbidden and fuck knows what else. He has to restrain me with one arm around my middle and force me with the other arm across my back—and that isn't even the half of it. Oh no, oh no, that isn't the most incredibly awful and unbelievable part. That award goes to the way it feels after he does it, and my bare ass is in the air with everything right out in the open. Not just my bare ass either but the slippery seam between, so exposed I can hardly stand to think about it.

But the moment I do it just…happens.

I come. I come in great heavy pulses, moaning into the only thing available—his still-tense and restraining arm. I just turn my head and do it, while my body does even more embarrassing things. I rut at the air like a dog in heat and squirm and buck, and all the while he makes it worse because he holds me. He holds me so tightly, as though he knows that's what I need. He just understands, he completely understands.

Or so I think, until he speaks into the still heavy silence.

"Did you just come because I pulled your panties down?" he says, that amused incredulity so thick in his voice I could drown in it. I *do* drown in it, in all honesty.

I sink into it right up to my embarrassed eyeballs, and refuse to ever come back out.

Chapter Seven

THE TRICK IS in thinking of a good reason why I would want to stay in his bathroom forever. Sadly for me, however, I sort of fail after minute five. He calls through the door—in a tone I could swear is still highly entertained by my sexual weirdness—and all I can come up with is *I need to brush my hair*. Despite the fact that hair brushing takes about three seconds and I do not even have anything to do it with. There is a flimsy comb in the medicine cabinet above the sink, and nothing else.

Which seems pretty unjust to me. He must need more than a comb. I doubt an industrial rake would get through his wild tangles, so why is his bathroom so bereft? And more important: Why am I worried about the lack of convincing hair-grooming items in here when he obviously knows that brushing is not what I'm worried about? I'm worried that he (a) thinks I'm some kind of gauche, knock-kneed idiot who can barely get through the beginning of sex without fucking it up and (b) now that he knows this, everything will come to a screeching halt.

It already *has* come to a screeching halt. As soon as he started laughing I had to make my excuses and flee to the bathroom. Now I'm trapped in here, instead of enjoying the carnal delights I just know were in the cards. If I'd simply kept a level head he would have been fucking me by now. I think he wanted to—or at the very least was in enough of a lust haze to go through with the whole thing.

But that lust haze is long gone.

"Come on, Rosie, come out so we can talk."

He wants to talk. Most probably about me and my hair-trigger vagina.

Nothing kills a lust daze faster than a hair-trigger vagina.

"I need to whizz, okay? Can you just let me whizz in peace?"

"I would if you were really whizzing, but we both know you're not."

"How would you know that I'm not?"

"Because my toilet is a thousand years old and practically echoes when the slightest thing drips on its ancient porcelain basin. All I hear in there is you desperately trying to find something to stall over."

Man he's good.

"Maybe I'm just really nosy."

"You'd rather be nosy than stalling for no reason at all?"

"I'd rather be neither of those two guys, but you're giving me very little option."

"Okay I tell you what—you can be a woman who is going to come out of the bathroom now so I can tell her that whole thing was not a big deal."

I pause before answering then.

Mainly because I adore him.

But partly because I feel silly having to say: "Was it really not?"

"It was actually kind of cool."

"Now you're just yanking my chain."

"Hand to God. And you can tell I'm serious too because I did not even make a joke about you saying *chain* there. I kept things on the level."

"Okay then, I'm coming out," I say, full of all the good intentions in the world. I open the door with confidence and all but stride into the room, ready to face whatever music he wants to now play. But then I see his face and horrible killer-clown music from a carnival of death starts tinkling away, and I pretty much lose any nerve I had. He just looks so wary—like I'm a bear who mauled him once and now wants to finish the job. When I manage to sidle over to the bed and sit down he practically moves to the other end of the room.

And then there are the things he says, once he gets there.

"So you been reading anything interesting lately?"

I think I come pretty close to throwing up my hands in defeat.

"See, I knew I totally fucked it up."

"You didn't fuck it up," he says, and to his credit he makes it seem convincing. He waves a hand and shakes his head in this bizarrely handsome way—one eye creased and near closed, lip slightly curled, beard brandished for maximum impact. It should really work.

It's just that it doesn't.

"But you were going to do other stuff and I just jumped the gun. I feel like a teenage boy creaming in my pants before the main event."

"I wasn't going to do anything good anyway."

"I bet it was. I bet it was awesome."

"A slight spanking is not that awesome. Frankly I'm relieved now I don't have to be such a cliche," he says, and even chuckles about it. I have no idea why though. He said the least funny thing in the world. In fact it is so not funny that my voice goes all weird and deep and wobbly when I reiterate for him.

"You were going to spank me."

"Just a little. With my hand," he says as though his hand is nothing when any fool can see otherwise.

You could be blind with a sex aversion to fingers and still understand, but as I am neither, I am in trouble. I have to point and ask, like some fool struck into inarticulacy by an innocent body part.

"That hand right there?"

"Yes this hand right here," he says, then *waves it at me*. He waves that awesome, enormous hand at me.

I feel like telling him he needs a permit to open-carry it.

"And then just like…open and hard against my ass."

"I guess you could describe it that way sure."

"How many times?"

"I have no idea," he says, because the evasion is not just in his eyes. It's clear in his words and actions too. He sits on the dresser, but he does it in the most awkward way possible. And as soon as it becomes clear that I can't stop watching his hands like a cat with a laser dot he tries to kind of…hide them a little. Or not know what to do with them. They seem as though they're not a part of him anymore, and he can't quite operate them or fit them any place.

Plus he appears to hate answering my next question.

"Maybe like ten?" I ask.

And he mumbles this:

"I guess maybe."

Which of course only makes me want to push harder.

"Or twenty," I say, because I am bad very bad.

I even *sound* like a bad girl.

"I doubt I would have gotten to twenty."

"But ten would probably be enough."

"Enough for what?" he asks, and now there is real suspicion in his voice. I can't really blame him, however. I'm suspicious of my motives too. After all, my tongue keeps curling up to touch my teeth and I appear to be clutching at myself under the pillow I don't remember pulling into my lap. None of that would look innocent at the best of times, and this is not the best of times.

This is a slow descent into the sort of weirdness I don't really mind.

"Enough to make my ass all red and sore."

"Probably yeah. Probably some," he says, because the further I go with this the more his vocabulary shrinks, apparently. He barely even manages the whole of that second *probably*, as though the things I tell him are sort of eating away at his power.

Not that I can stop.

I have to know.

"Do you think there would be a handprint?"

"I think we should change the subject."

"Please don't change the subject. I just want to hear, okay. If you're not going to do it now, I at least want to hear what it would be like."

"More than possibly painful."

"Uh-huh. So not sitting down for days then."

"As much as a week," he says, because he's quite clearly trying to put me off now. He sounds like an elderly doctor extolling the dangers of cigarettes. It's just too bad that I do not care about the dangers of cigarettes. That really, I don't consider any of this dangerous at all. It's making my face go very hot. And most of that embarrassment? Completely forgotten.

How can it be otherwise when he just said *a week*?

A week of blistering, squirmy agony.

"Oh my God."

"Every time you move you feel it."

"Oh yeah. Oh that sounds really…awful."

"That burning sting almost constantly—" he starts, but does not finish.

Mostly because I think he just realized the kind of effect he's actually having on me. I am definitely not responding like someone on the receiving end of a stern lecture about the dangers of being spanked. Instead

I seem to be slumping way, way, down on the bed, and my hands are doing things that I am sort of pretending they're not. If I just pretend they're not then he can just keep right on talking like that and I can keep right on listening and that hot ache I seem to be experiencing between my legs can continue building.

Maybe until I embarrass myself all over again.

Which actually sort of happens a second later, thanks to the faintly disbelieving question he then asks.

"Are you touching yourself under there?"

"No. No. That would be weird right? No."

"I wouldn't say weird. I would say horny."

"Horny seems just as bad. Like that teenage boy again."

"Yeah but it's not really the same for women."

"It feels like it might be," I say, then come pretty close to stopping.

That embarrassment is back, and it brought reinforcements.

Fortunately for me, however, he decides to take this opportunity to knock said reinforcements down.

"Well that's probably because you're the one fingering yourself under a pillow even as we talk about completely not-arousing things—which most likely seems pretty weird to you. Whereas I am the one who has to watch you getting all pink-cheeked and heavy-eyed with those perky little nipples sticking through your top and that slick sound going on as you do what I can only really guess at, which of course only makes it more agonizing and unbearable for me in pretty much every single way."

I mean, should I get up and applaud after that? It feels like my vagina really, really wants to. I can practically feel it straining at the material of my panties. He says the word *nipples* and this great hot thrum just sort of swells everything down there. I'm surprised I can't hear elastic snapping—but that may be down to what my hand does in the middle of the most arousing thing I've ever heard a man say.

I squeeze myself there.

Then sort of regret it. It makes my voice come out all wobbly, when I'm trying to answer in a calm and reasonable fashion.

"That sounds like kind of a good thing."

"It is kind of a good thing."

"You like me being excited?" I ask, despite knowing what the answer is. The thing is though…I just want to hear him say it out loud. I need to know that he wants me as much as I want him—but Christ I am not prepared for it when he says it. His tone dips a whole octave lower, and it was already pretty low to begin with. Sometimes when he talks I feel the vibrations between my legs, so this kind of puts me over the edge. *I do*, he says, and then I really just have to do something about my own boiling-over arousal. I know it will make me look lewd as fuck and sound even worse than it already does, but I don't care. I don't even care if it makes him back away again, or start talking about some other nonsexual thing.

I need to properly touch myself. Not just over the top of my panties but underneath, oh God, I want to touch underneath, and when I do, when I ease my eager fingers over that slippery seam…it feels so good I pretty much forget about where I am and who I'm with and what I should or should not be doing. All that matters is that thick bloom of pleasure—the one that intensifies tenfold when I just ever so slightly stroke over my clit. Just a little, just slowly, but *slowly* and *little* are more than enough.

They make me arch my back and almost moan.

And say things I do not mean to say.

"Want to see too?"

"What do you think?"

"I think I'll show you if you spank me for it," I tell him, and for a second feel sure he will say no. It feels too much like a seedy deal to really persuade him, and especially with this background of greedy masturbation. I can hear myself now, never mind him making it out. And I know how I must look. My eyes are practically slits and my mouth won't stay closed. I've arched my back so much my tits seem obscene and that pillow is barely covering anything up by this point.

It's not just the noise.

It's the jerky motion. The spread of my legs, the way I'm shivering and rocking, the smell of sex in the air. If he backed off over our ages or the handcuffs or the fact that I came over the slightest thing, he's got to do it for this. I can almost hear him saying it: *maybe we could try something a little less scary.*

So when he says the following:

"Okay. You be the slut. I'll be the guy who punishes you for it."

It kind of has a big effect on me.

A really, really big effect on me.

"Oh my God oh my God I'm gonna come."

"Yeah that strikes the right sort of tone," he says, but only because he thinks this is pretend. Strangely though, it's not that embarrassing to correct him.

"No I'm *actually* gonna come again," I say, and this time I find myself almost revelling in his response. I like the shock in his voice when he asks me if I'm kidding. I like the expression on his face, all lust blown and sort of slack. And maybe, yeah maybe it's not *just* the idea of his excitement, or the fact that he enjoys mine. There might also be a little frisson over the thought of being the thing he wanted to pretend I was.

A slut, a horny no-good slut who comes over nothing while he watches.

And moans really loudly while doing it. "Ohhhh man," I tell him, and the thrill is just electric. It sends my body into spasms and makes me want to do even naughtier things—though to my delight he gets to all of them first. "Move that pillow out of the way so I can see you being a little trollop," he says, and he does it so well I have no idea if he is just playing or not. It sounds real.

And more important:

It *feels* real.

I feel ordered to do something, to the point where it is almost impossible to disobey. As soon as he speaks I move the pillow aside, and I do not close my legs before I do it. I keep them spread with my skirt all rucked up and my fingers so busy on my just-about-bursting clit, so close to going over that just the idea of how that must look almost makes it happen. In fact, I think it probably would have done if it were not for his response to it—which is not what I expect at all.

I'm always thinking of him backing off, and instead he suddenly grabs my hand.

He stops me, before I can do it. More than that really—he pulls my fingers free of my panties in a way that makes my body scream in frustration. Hell, it makes me *actually* scream in frustration—or least ask him a rather desperate-sounding question.

"No, what are you—" I start to say.

And then he decides to cut me off with this:

"I'll teach you to be such a tease. Get on your hands and knees."

After which I think I possibly pass out. At the very least I swoon, if swooning actually means your whole body goes rigid, and your eyes get really big, and excitement almost strangles you to death. For about half an hour all I do is stare at him, but staring doesn't make things any better. It just tells me how hot he looks when he pretends to be an asshole—in part because he does it so well. He looks mad as fuck and twice as fierce, those eyes like hot coals burning right into the middle of my body.

Only the way he waits tells me the truth underneath.

That little silence he leaves, for me to fill up with my safe word.

And that I just about leave in the dust. I do what he says down to the letter—shakily and clumsily, true, but I get there all the same. I face away from him on all fours, and as soon as I do I understand why he demanded it. Being on my back in front of him was blissful. But being like this is a goddamned revelation. I want to moan as soon as I'm in position, head so full of all the things he can probably see it almost drowns me. I bet my underwear is all soaked and pulled so taut over my swollen pussy.

But nothing beats him actually pointing some of that out.

"Pull those wet panties down," he says.

And that's when the shaking starts.

And the begging, of course.

"Please, please just…please," I say, but sadly I can't quite get to the part where I explain what my *please* is about.

Which is doubly unfortunate, because he really wants to know.

"Please just what? Please just let you come?" he asks, and just when I go to nod or maybe make a sound that seems like it could be a yes, he leans in real close and whispers low and hot in my ear, "Horny little sluts don't get to come."

Then just in case that was not thrilling enough, he takes it upon himself to do what he just demanded. He starts pulling down my panties—just like before in the store only not half so careful and deliberate about it. This is rough and heated, with a soundtrack of his harsh breathing over the top. He sounds like an animal, I think, like that werewolf I once thought of, and it makes me crazy.

But not as much as his next words.

"Horny little sluts get punished."

Oh, the second he says those words…

I think I drift off into some other realm entirely. Everything goes all still and silent and weird inside me, and nothing else exists except for the sense of the thing he is going to do. *He is going to do it now*, I think, and then he does and everything breaks. The person I was disintegrates, and leaves behind the sort of girl who sings inside for that short, sharp shock.

And for the thing he demands after the fact.

"Say you're sorry," he says, and my mind greedily flutters over all the things I should do it for. I was such a dirty girl, such a bad girl, such an overeager come-hungry embarrassment. I wanted to fuck him the first night we spent together, and all my thoughts have been of nothing else since. I had an orgasm over nothing and masturbated right in front of him, and all of it makes my apology so big and bursting.

"I'm so sorry," I say and that's when this game really gets me. Not in the physicality of it, not in the spanking or the touching or the sense that I really did do something wrong, but in the rush of my own shame as it washes away.

"Say it again," he tells me, and I all but shout it.

"I am, I'm sorry," I say, as my body gives in to this bliss. Orgasm hits me so hard it leaves me a wreck, but even as it does I understand one thing very clearly. I see it in the eye of this storm: now that I've had a taste I will never want to stop.

I am never, ever going to want to stop.

Chapter Eight

I KIND OF imagine that nothing can ever top what we just did, but to be honest everything that follows is even more heavenly than the stuff that came before. He puts some scratchy old music on his record player, like the soundtrack to forbidden affairs in French movies that I had no idea could really be a thing. And after a while of just being there together, he just goes ahead and starts braiding my hair. I could honestly say *I love you* over him braiding my hair.

And then he has to go and spoil it with more completely pointless worrying.

"See what I mean about how I get when I do things like that?" he asks, right in the middle of me almost falling asleep to the strains of Edith Piaf.

Can he not see me falling asleep to the strains of Edith Piaf?

"I see that it was awesome."

"Even though I called you a slut?"

"*Especially* because you called me a slut."

"So you don't see a problem with it?"

"Unless by problem you mean: made me come harder than I ever have in my whole life," I say, but still it doesn't sink in. I'm starting to think nothing will, considering the words that are coming out of my mouth and the things that I just did. Plus there is the current state of me. I look like I just got a seventeen-hour massage from four massive Swedish guys. I can barely sit up straight—though that isn't really a problem.

He provides an awesome bed for me to lie against.

"I was thinking more the part where I punished you for being one."

"Yeah but you did that mostly because you knew I wanted you to."

"Well yeah, but I can hardly say I hated it."

"I fail to see how you not hating it is a bad thing."

"Maybe it means I secretly feel that way."

"So you really think sluts should be punished for being horny?"

"Of course not. I hope not. What if I do?" he asks, the hand that was so pleasantly playing with my hair now still. The voice that was turning my bones to syrup suddenly fraught with actual concern, instead of just the idle discussion I thought we were having.

I at least thought I was getting through to him, but apparently not.

"If you did I doubt giving girls orgasms would help you."

"That is a very good point."

"Or that you would braid my hair afterward."

"Probably not, no."

"And you wouldn't be having this conversation with me in the first place. Either you would be in such deep denial that you'd pretend everything was totally cool, or I would be the one crying over you calling me a slut while you sneered over what a little baby I was being," I say, and *now* I think I might have gotten somewhere. The hand moves over my hair again, and when it does it just feels *so* tender.

And when he speaks, he sounds that way too.

"I think the fact that my heart just tried to eat itself over the idea of doing that last thing is probably a good sign. All I want to do is, like, cuddle you and sip wine over dinner and take baths together," he says, quite possibly because he is awesome. Not only is he some kind of sex wizard, but he also apparently wants to do all the things I've always dreamed of and assumed were not in the cards for someone like me. I am a mess. Messes do not get scenes from a montage in a romantic movie about a married couple.

They don't even get married, unless the marriage is in Las Vegas to a drug dealer called Biff. And even then it has to be annulled three seconds later because it turns out he is already married to the ten hookers he owns, of which he would like you to be one.

Yeah, that sounds more like my future. Or maybe my mom's life.

Which probably explains why I turn my head, to make sure he is not just teasing me.

And sound so excited, when I realize he is totally not.

"You want to take a *bath* together," I say.

Then just about die when he does not take it away.

"Well, sure. You really want to do that?"

"Are you kidding me? Get that thing running, dude," I say, and then watch in far too giddy a way as he actually goes ahead and does. He gets bath salts out, and makes me pick a scent—as though I have any idea about the non-sense that goes into these sorts of things. I've barely had anything like it in my own life, never mind with another person who totally knows what to do. And he *does* really know what to do.

He lights a candle and sets it on the side of the tub. He gets a bottle of wine from the fridge in the kitchen upstairs and pours it into wineglasses. There are fluffy towels and much more sensuous music, and just when I think it could not get any better—not in a million years not ever—he stops mid-running-back-and-forth in front of a dazedly grinning me, and raises both his fists in a kind of triumph.

"I can't *believe* I finally get to do this," he says.

Because amazingly, it seems that he's never done it before either. I guess he's just really imagined it a lot, but never had someone to do it with—a fact that staggers me until I remember what he said about his past. I might think of a mythical future where I have to marry a pimp, but that could well be an actual chapter from his life.

He was forced to marry Biff in Las Vegas.

And now all of this is going to make up for it.

Oh man, am I ever going to make up for it.

"What are you doing?"

"Taking off your clothes. It's kind of a requirement of bath taking."

"I know, but you seem to be doing it in less of a requirement sort of way and more as a really superarousing kind of thing. A really, really arousing kind of thing," he says, and though he has a point about the way I'm doing it—I seem to be roaming my hands around under his cardigan more than actually undoing anything—I find I can't really focus on that.

I have to focus on that one word he said, instead.

"Oh my God. Say that again."

"Say what again?"

"Arousing."

"You like that word, huh?"

"I like the idea of you being turned on," I say, even though it must be obvious. My voice comes out all husky and my hands are twice as roam-happy now. I could swear I just accidentally slid inside the sleeve of his cardigan all the way down to the elbow—but to be fair I have other reasons for that.

His arms are fucking *incredible*.

They are twists of thick rope. You could haul in gigantic boats using them. I almost start tearing off his shirt just so I can get a closer look, and restrain myself only because of the thing he tells me. Though really, restraining myself is not what happens. He says:

"Then you should probably know I've been turned on since around oh, eight thousand years ago. My cock could probably hammer nails—but the fact that all of that is true does not really alter what we are supposed to do here."

And then I think my body just seizes up. I go to respond three times and completely fail, so end up just standing there with my mouth hanging open. *He said his cock could hammer nails*, my stunned mind informs me in hushed tones, despite the fact that hushed tones should not be needed. He thrashed my bare ass a couple of hours ago. This should not be so exciting or shocking or whatever it is that I can feel thrumming through me. I should be prepared for him to talk like a nymphomaniac pirate.

But I know why I'm not.

It's because up until this point he gave almost no indication that he even had a cock, never mind a stiff one. Other than heavy breathing—which could well have been part of the show—he might as well have been dead down there. He has been a model of restraint when it comes to his desires, to the point where I feel sort of ashamed of myself.

And not in the good way.

The bad way, where I am a selfish asshole.

I can't even offer to do anything to him. My vocal cords are still in as much shock as the rest of me. I have to wait until he senses that I have broken down and points out what we were supposed to do, before I can get myself together and respond.

"We were going to take a nice, mellow bath together," he says.

Then the paralysis gives way just a little.

"You want to take a nice, mellow bath together even though your cock could hammer nails?" I ask, and to be honest even hearing myself speak the words is exciting.

I get that thick pulse between my legs, barely an hour after my last orgasm.

"I appreciate that this is unusual in a world where men frequently answer innocent questions on dating websites with pictures of their dicks."

"It's unusual after you just spanked me."

"Well yeah, that too, but stay with me here. I was thinking that we just...you know...relax and talk and have some wine, *in between* the sexual encounters. What do you say?"

What *can* I say? He just said that completely cool thing about dick pics and dating sites. He wants to do slow, romantic stuff instead of immediately yanking me onto his cock by my hair. Which admittedly I might like when it is him doing the yanking, but under normal circumstances is much less kinky and a great deal more awful and nightmarish. Once some guy did it and almost took out my right eye. He said he was aiming for my mouth, but when you're using someone's head as a joystick it obviously gets difficult.

In fact, all of sex was difficult for me before this, so maybe I should just let him keep doing whatever he thinks is best. It could be his patience that really makes it good. Perhaps I'm not being a selfish asshole by allowing this to all unfold the way he suggests. And I am excited to try something that couples who are massively into each other usually do.

It makes me think that's what we are—a thought that seems mildly ridiculous until we start doing this whole mellow thing. He says "Okay, so we can undress each other but no sexy touching or horny kissing or any of that stuff all right?" And I, like an idiot, agree. I even think it will be fine, until we start peeling off items of clothing. After which, it is not fine at all.

Mostly because in the absence of sex, everything somehow *becomes* sex. It's like sex rushes in to fill the sex void. Previously innocent actions like removing a cardigan somehow turn into these agonizing, hour-long productions of incredibly erotic plays. Even the laugh he gives me because he has to turn so I can get it off becomes exciting. It breaks the silence like a moan of ecstasy in the middle of mass, and everything just devolves from there.

Of course it does.

That was just his outerwear.

Now I've got to get his shirt off. He's got to get my shirt off. Eventually we're going to get to bras and briefs and oh God, why did I agree to this? I feel as though we're peeling off skin again, and underneath I'm still all raw and wired. Each time he brushes a bared part of me I go weak. I want to sit down.

At the very least I want to kiss him, but he said no to that too.

Or could I just maybe give him a little one?

A soft, nonhorny one must be okay—and especially in light of the way he unlaces my sneakers. He kneels down to do it, and I swear I think my heart becomes a cliche. It skips a beat, it starts hammering, it loses its place in the book it's been reading. Surely it must be appropriate here. He even glances up at me after he's slipped them off, like some prince from a really hairy and weird version of *Cinderella*.

And so I just do it. I lean down and press my lips to his, without thinking of what the consequences will be. I'm just worried about seeming too sexual for this little web of sensuousness we're supposed to be weaving, and don't consider that the opposite might happen. I go in out of what I think is hunger for him.

Then get this long, slow, soft thing that leaves me utterly wrecked. All these emotions start happening, and especially after he responds. He reaches up and touches the braid he made. He pulls me down to sit, and only after he does do I realize I'm sitting on his crooked knee. I'm sitting on his knee and I'm kissing him and he's kissing me and for the first time in my life I truly understand what romance is.

It's being so sweet on someone you barely know you are until it sneaks up on you. It comes in like a thief of my heart, and as soon as it does I sort of want to hide. I stand up too suddenly and back away too fast, heart jumping and jumping in my chest. I have to grab the glass of wine on the edge of the bath and take a great gulp to calm myself down, but when I do, it doesn't really help as much as I expect.

Mostly because the wine is not wine at all.

"There's no alcohol in this."

"Were you desperately needing it to be?"

"Well, no not exactly but…"

"But you were kind of desperately needing it to be," he says, and then all I can do is just stare at him helplessly. How does he know this stuff? How does he just talk about it like he's taking it in stride?

"Sorry, honey—I'm not real big on drinking."

"Not even the occasional beer?"

"Not even the occasional *light* beer."

"But you have those herbal things though."

"Oh no, you don't want those."

"Why not? They sound pretty harmless," I say, because really what I'm thinking of here is that stuff you get from the health store that makes your teeth green. Instead of the expression he gives me—all eyebrows and head tilting and coupled with a cute little hand seesaw. And the thing he then says. Oh man, I love the thing he then says.

"Yeah probably because I *said* herbal things but what I actually meant was marijuana."

"And you think I'm going to say whoa no way, you drug pusher?"

"More like I would feel kind of drug pusher-y."

"Go get the pot. Get the pot. Get it. Get it. Get the pot," I say.

I even point in the direction the pot is hopefully in.

And that is how we end up naked at opposite ends of his tub, glowing in the heat and gleaming with the soapy bubbles he put in, giggling over the fact that his legs are so long he has to hang them over the sides to fit in here with me. I honestly have no idea why either of us thought this was a good plan, but boy does it feel like one when I get another hit of that amazing whatever-it-is.

He kisses curls of smoke into my mouth and I just drift away with him.

"Feeling better now?"

"I feel fine it's just…"

"You don't have to explain. First I kidnap you, then I indoctrinate you into a world of kinky weirdness, and now here I am getting you to do drugs…" he says, in that laid-back but somehow utterly hilarious way of his. He waves the hand holding the joint and does all of this great work with his eyebrows and is just somehow ten times as attractive because of it.

Though that may well be the drugs talking.

Or the fact that I can see a hell of a lot of his naked body. He kind of climbed in without me getting too much of a glimpse, but now there is plenty to take in. Like his shoulders, which are just as enormous as I suspected. And his arms that could belong to a man who spends his days working in a granite pit, if granite pits were a real thing. Which I want them to be, so I can look them up later and better picture him carving out great hunks of the stuff with bare hands and his bare arms and his bare chest.

Maybe while sweating a whole hell of a lot.

"Shut *up*. None of that is even remotely accurate."

"What are you talking about? It is exactly accurate."

"But you make it sound like a harrowing tale about my descent into debauchery at the hands of a criminal mastermind instead of you know…like…all sweet and stuff."

"You think this is all sweet and stuff?" he asks, and though I don't think his incredulity is the bad sort I still kind of want to take it back. You know, just in case it is.

"Well not now that you've said it like that."

"I said it super normally. I think you're just scared," he says, after which I simply have to correct him. I have to.

Even though I 100 percent know he is right.

"*I'm* the scared one? You were totally the one with the scaring."

"That is not an accurate grammar…thing."

"Neither is that—you just said grammar thing!"

"My point still stands."

"What point still stands? The one about grammar things?"

"The one about you being scared. Of feelings," he says, as though that was just the most obvious thing in the world. Which it was—I just pretended otherwise so I wouldn't have to answer the charge.

Now I've got to throw it back at him, somehow.

"I am not scared of feelings. *You're* scared of feelings," I say, but it just comes out so silly. I think I might be laughing as I let the words out, and he is definitely laughing once he hears them. No one could mistake his amusement for anything else. It's big and comforting and cool, just like him.

Plus he finishes it by suddenly leaning toward me. Features partly obscured by trailing smoke but so beautiful my breath kind of catches—the way men usually do over women. I have no choice but to do what he wants when he asks it of me, even though I feel sort of nervous about what it might be. "Come here a second I have a secret to tell you," he says, and my heart starts to beat through my skin.

You know that thing, when you can see it?

I can see it. I see my heart like a hummingbird just under the surface, as I lean in.

"What is the secret you want to tell me?" I say, voice as faint as snow falling. Eyes too big and too eager to devour him, every part of me vibrating over what I know is coming. I can tell by the way he looks at me, and yet even so I'm somehow not prepared.

Though in my defense, no one could ever be for this.

"I am totally one hundred percent falling for you. Like seriously head-over-heels crazy about everything you do, thinking about you night and day, missing you even when you're here, wanting-to-climb-under-your-skin completely overboard for you, and I have zero problems admitting it. But I know that when we kissed back then— you know that kiss that felt like falling into a fantasy of what kissing is—the first thing you did was try to down a glass of wine and then ask me for pot. So you don't have to admit that's what happened if you don't want to, but all I'm saying is it won't be a shock to me if you do."

He has zero problems admitting, I think.

He misses me when I'm here, I think.

And then I just have to sit there for about five years, in total silence. Well, I say total silence, but to be honest my heart is pounding so hard it sort of seems like the neighbors should be pounding on the walls to tell me to turn it off. Not that I can blame it though, considering that he just gave me a speech I've never even seen aimed at Anne Hathaway in her last romantic movie.

How am I getting something better than Anne Hathaway in a romantic movie?

My hair is nowhere near as great as hers. My cheeks look like I store nuts for the winter. I try to have conversations about beings from other planets and I lapse into stunned silence after awesome speeches—despite the fact

that I definitely feel the same way. I just want to do something weird now, like rub my face all over his face. This
alarm keeps going off in my head, and the alarm is almost
constantly bleating *he is your soul mate he is your soul mate*
even though I could swear that soul mates are not a real
thing.

People just invented it so they could sell crystals and
incense.

Oh my God, I don't think people invented it to sell
crystals and incense. It seems like a real thing, made
up of beards and sexual electricity and long talks about
absolutely nothing. Wearing handcuffs as bracelets and
being in bathtubs and knowing—just *knowing*—with
every fiber of my being after five fucking seconds of being
in his company. He is the one.

It's just that I totally fucking fail at *articulating* that
he is the one.

I downplay it, like the ridiculous coward I am.

"I think I might love you a little bit. Is that weird?"

Christ, I sound twelve years old.

I feel twelve years old—like a kid who has no ability to
properly identify what this is. I must be mistaken in some
way, or just be acting the way I did when I had a crush
on Edward Norton aged ten. I was so sure I was going to
one day marry him, and live on an island he had bought
just for me.

And that is how ridiculous this feels.

Until he just casually tells me:

"I would probably be a hypocrite if I said yes."

He doesn't even balk at all.

Honestly his earthy practicality is fucking awesome.

"So then I guess you kind of love me a little bit."

"I think I kind of love you a *lot*, but probably I should save that declaration for our wedding that no doubt we will attend tomorrow before you give birth to our seventeen children on Wednesday," he says, because apparently he knows just what I need is to stop worrying about how absurd all of this is.

I need him to make fun of it too.

I need to laugh, and I do.

"It could be just the pot talking."

"This pot is barely more than a cigarette."

"Are you kidding me? You're kidding me right?"

"These bath salts are probably more potent."

"Shut up—you said grammar thing."

"I guess I'm just high on love."

"And what am I high on?"

"Even more love than that," he says, and then I just kiss him. No thinking about it, no worrying about it, no sense that I'm making some epic blunder. I just put my mouth on his and get my hands all in his hair and push right up against him. And for a while, he pushes right back. I get one big hand spanning my bare shoulder blades and his tongue doing crazy-good things to mine, and all of it is just so completely amazing and glorious and good that I barely think anything of it when he pulls away.

Who would, when things are this good?

Chapter Nine

EVERY TIME I return I expect things to have changed. We never really exchanged such soft, sweet words. My heart didn't actually try to escape out of my chest. He isn't that into me. When I go back I will get the cold shoulder, the big explanation, the brush-off.

And then I get to the store and he just wraps me in wonderfulness.

Twice he has dinner ready for me when I get there, as though dinner is just a thing I deserve. I get pasta he made from scratch in the tiny kitchen at the back of the store, followed by dessert from the bakery down the street. And even when there is no dinner, he gives me things I could absolutely die over. His taste in music is amazing, and even better coming out of that busted old record player. It makes me feel like this is something that someone wrote a song about, in the seventies. I go back to my place with my head full of "Cecilia" by Simon and Garfunkel, or "Cry Baby" by Janis Joplin.

And that isn't even the best part.

No, the best part is the *reading*. All of the reading that he does for me, right when I least expect it. I'm just standing there watching him inventory books, and he suddenly opens one and starts reciting a passage. Sometimes when we lie together on his bed he will get whatever is on his nightstand and tell me something good he found inside.

And better yet: occasionally the something good will be in *German*. He reads things to me in German, then chuckles over the fact that I ever thought it would sound amazing. I have to explain to him that my heart kind of wants to eat his face, after hearing him saying *ich* and *liebe* and *dich*. I have to say it back, because I know what he's really telling me.

I see what he does when he reads these passages aloud.

He says what he feels, in someone else's words.

He tells me what Jane thinks of being torn asunder from Rochester, and how Arthur longs for Little Dorritt, and oh everything is so good that I just let myself be relieved. Even when he makes excuses to not go too far or push too much, I don't really sense a problem. I just think he will come around, if I can hit on the right thing. Persuade him in some subtle way, like maybe with a kiss on the cheek after a particularly stirring rendition of an ee cummings poem. Or hand between his legs, when that gets no results.

Yeah, the hand between his legs seems to work a little better—though at first he still sort of tries to resist. "Is it really such a bad thing to just want to date?" he says.

But I persevere—and I'm glad I do.

Because the second I redouble my efforts, something definitely shifts. I lick his ear and feel him stiffen and then relax, and that hand he had on my waist kind of slides down a little. Not too much and not too quickly, but the move is there. All I need is another four hours, and this fixation on just dating he has will fall by the wayside.

Either that, or he will just suddenly break.

Lord in heaven, I am not prepared for the sudden break. He just makes a noise like a starving man falling on a frosted cake, half-frustrated and half-laughing and half-disapproving, followed by something that makes me damn near lose my mind. He doesn't just *spread* me out. He *pins me down*. He holds my hands above my head and says that I am so bad—two words that are practically a dog whistle to me now.

I go hot all over at just the sound.

And then again when he adds:

"I think I'm going to have to teach you a lesson."

Oh, I do love his lessons. I spend most of my time daydreaming about them. Last night I masturbated twice in a row with the idea of him tying me up sort of singing in my head, even though I've never masturbated twice in a row in my life. Usually I go to sleep after one round, but one round was not enough for a fantasy like that.

And especially when it isn't really a fantasy at all.

It's something he really does.

In fact, he does *better* than that. He thinks of details I almost never do, like maybe not using anything to hold me in place at all. "Here's what's going to happen," he says, and then my breath decides to take a vacation from my body as he lays it all out. "You're going to take hold of that bed frame above your head with both hands. And no matter what I do, or say, or you might want, you absolutely cannot let go. Think of it like your hands are held there with invisible bonds, and the only thing that can break them is my say-so.

"You got that?"

Oh God, yeah.

I got it.

I've got it so hard my hands are wrapped around the wrought iron before he finishes speaking. I'm already utterly turned on, and it shows. Even to me it shows. When I glance down I can see my stiff nipples poking through the thin material of my T-shirt—made worse by the position I seem to have taken up. I think my back may be a little arched and my legs are not exactly politely laid together. One of them is still crooked over his and the other is as far away as it can get without splitting me in two.

None of which would be so bad, if it were not for my skirt.

Yeah, my skirt is kind of up around my hips somewhere.

And maybe I might have also forgotten to wear a particular item of clothing.

"You walked all the way here without any underwear on?"

"Oops, do I have no underwear on? I could have sworn I remembered."

"Oh you are a pistol. Probably pointed right at my head. And I think it just went off."

"Yeah but to be fair I am really, really…not sorry at all."

"You will be after I punish you. Because I got to be honest, Rosie. The penalty for walking around without panties is pretty steep."

"Am I supposed to say no, please, anything but that?"

"You'll be saying it for real pretty soon."

"Promises, promises. You talk big but…" I say then shrug.

But oh man he makes me pay for that immediately. The moment I let my shoulder lift in that cheeky sort of way, he just gets ahold of me. He gets ahold of me really firmly, right around my waist, and just when I think that is the extent of this lesson he goes one further.

He runs those hands all the way inside my T-shirt.

All the way inside, and *over my breasts*. At which point, I realize something in a rather shocking flood. He has never touched me like that before. He has never cupped me there as though he wants to enjoy my body. He keeps himself largely detached from his own desire to fondle me, to the point where I was starting to think it might not exist.

But oh no, it exists.

And it makes me go limp.

It forces a gasp from my parted lips.

"But what? I talk big but what?"

"I don't know. I just lost my train of thought," I say.

Almost entirely because he is now just ever so slightly tugging at my erect nipples with his fingers and his thumbs.

"Uh-huh. See, I think you imagine punishment is just slapping a little ass, or maybe getting out a belt, or being rough. But it's really not. Punishment can be as easy as making someone stay right where they are while you drive them out of their fucking minds. Because believe me when I say this—I am very, very good at driving women out of their minds."

"You are?" I ask, and though I want to sound less incredulous about it, I find I am really struggling. In my defense, however, it is really hard to be sure about anything, when someone is still stroking your insanely sensitive breasts.

Over and over, he does it.

Over and over and around and oh God.

"Oh you thought by BDSM I meant that I excelled at being a brute? No, no, no. What I really know how to do is something called *pleasure control*. You ever heard of that? It's pretty straightforward. I just do a whole bunch of amazing things to you until you're a sobbing, gibbering wreck. And then when you finally break down and beg me to let you come, I go ahead and don't let you come some more. Sound good?"

"Sounds fantastic. Please hurry up and do it," I say, but now I'm the one talking big. In truth, that speech he just gave is turning my insides to some sort of jelly. I can feel it oozing out of my pores, one vital organ at a time.

And even more so, after he elaborates with this:

"Great! In that case I think we'll start out with a little prep work."

I mean, what exactly is prep work? It sounds like something insane doctors do, and that's *before* he returns with the tools he needs to do it. After he does it moves all the way from strange to kind of scary, though not exactly in the way I'm used to. This is a different kind of fear than the one I get when I realize I sent the wrong document to Professor Hendricks or almost fall down a flight of stairs. This is riddled through the middle with these odd little tingles, and though I try to stay still I know I'm squirming. I'm practically rocking on the bed with my legs still completely spread, and things stay that way even after he really lets me get a look at the thing in his hand.

It's actually a straight razor, I think, just like he said to me before.

Then I let out a little sound, to go alongside all the shaky breathing and the hip rolling. Honestly, by the time he gets around to explaining, I'm already half-gone. The words themselves are really just the icing on the cake.

"See when you strip a pussy of all that hair, it usually gets twice as sensitive. I mean it's not an exact science or anything, but I think the results will still prove my point. Unless you have any objections," he says, and at that point I sort of want to say yeah.

I've never been nude down there. I've always had a little protective covering, and I kind of want to keep it that way.

But thankfully my trust in him saves me.

"Go ahead," I tell him, in spite of my nervousness. And by God, am I glad I do. I expect it to be a little awkward and regret inducing—a thing I have to get past to move on to more exciting stuff. Instead of what I should have understood from the off: this is the exciting stuff.

Even the smallest, most innocuous parts of this are the exciting stuff...like the shaving foam, for example. He uses this thick, creamy soap that he sort works into a lather, and of course he doesn't just smear it all over me.

He works it between my legs, in the most agonizing, deliberate way possible. He knows exactly what he is easing that foam over and precisely how it feels when it does. On the outer edges of my cunt it tingles and teases, barely there no matter how thickly he spreads it on. And then when he moves between my lips, when he finds my clit with his end-less circles, the sensation switches to something heavier.

Suddenly the soap doesn't seem so light anymore.

It seems dense and everywhere all at once. I can feel every inch of my swollen bud beneath that creamy coat-ing, just aching and aching away. A little more of this and I think I could come—and that is the point where I realize how much trouble I'm in. He has barely done anything, and I'm already thinking about an orgasm he's never going to let me have.

In fact, the very second it seems like I might, he takes his hand away.

Worse than that: he mocks me for it.

"Already? Boy oh boy are you going to have a hard time here, sweetheart," he says, and then I love him and hate him all at the same time. I want to let go of the frame right then and there and go further than I dared before. Drag him down on top of me and make him do a thou-sand rude things. Suck his cock and fuck his face and just anything, anything at all, *anything*.

But I know why I don't.

It's because now he has that razor in his hand. And oh God, when he opens it up. He looks like a sadistic doctor from the nineteenth century, which sounds awful, I know, but does things to my insides that I didn't think were possible. My heart starts banging against my rib cage. My breath is coming like someone is sawing something in my throat. I feel pretty sure I'm going to pass out the second he touches me with that thing.

Only then he does, and I do something else instead.

I call out his name. I really, really call out his name. I bet people can hear it in France, but what can I do? He draws that thing through the foam as though carving out a work of art. Just the way he holds it—with his fingers braced into this glorious arch—is enough to give me all of the feelings. But then there's the sense of it barely skimming my oversensitized skin, and the strange relief that rushes in after each stroke.

It's like someone lifting a weight I didn't realize I was carrying.

It almost makes me cry, which seems silly on the face of it, but less so underneath. I mean, when have I ever trusted anyone like this in my whole life? And if I have, I can say with all certainty that they then let me down. My life is pretty much a patchwork of people who failed me in some way.

But not Han.

He doesn't even fail me with a razor blade against my skin. He finishes up and there is my pretty pink pussy, all soft and smooth and exposed in a way that sends shivers right the way through me. I sort of want to close my legs when I see it, yet at the same time I can hardly stop staring. I squirm around just to get a better look, and stop only when it occurs to me that he is very quiet.

Very quiet, and very bright-eyed—the way people sometimes get when they have a fever. He's burning up, I think, and I can tell why. Any fool would know it, considering the way he's looking at my bare cunt. Maybe he thought when he started this that it would only be me he affected. That he would drive me wild and that would be the end of it.

But I can see now that this is not the case.

I can still push him, from this position of weakness. I just have to work out how. I just have to lean a little harder until he breaks—a thing that seems hard on the face of it, but not so much once he really starts. Oh, once he really starts I can see desire all over him. "You want to see your sweet little pussy," he says, and I note that he says *sweet*. I note that he sounds hoarse when he does it. "You want to see how wet you are already," he says.

But the word *wet* comes out far thicker than anything else in that sentence. Like he slows down over it, to really savor every inch. I'm wet, he made me all wet, and if I just moan and spread my legs a little wider…if I let my mind drift to the things he might do next…

"Oh look at you just making a mess all over yourself. You really are a horny thing, huh?" he tells me, and then I know I have him then. The only problem is: he also has me.

"Well, let's see what we can do about making that way, way, way worse."

And he means it too.

Christ, does he ever mean it. He gets the scissors and cuts off my top—you know just for that intense callback to the thing I spend nights salivating over—and once that's done he decides the best course of action is to run his eyes all over my naked body. Greedily, heatedly, like he not only enjoys what he sees, but wants me to understand that he does. Then just in case the gaze alone is not enough, he goes and tells me.

What kind of man tells you that he thinks your body is hot?

Apart from this totally amazing one, of course.

"Man I could just eat you up—those curves, honey, those curves could drive a man to distraction. And that skin…never seen anything so soft and creamy seeming. Just makes me want to taste," he says, so low and intense for a second I almost think he might. He even leans down a little like he's going to, those lips sent from hell parting around all kinds of sensitive things.

And then just as it seems like he's there, just as I arch a little more to get my tight nipple close enough…that's when he leans back, like the total bastard he is.

"But I think maybe you need a little more priming before we get to the main event," he says, in a way that is definitely designed to give me a lot of frantic thoughts. Like: How am I meant to cope with another thing before the main event? Is the other thing going to be worse? And if it is, then what in God's name is the main event going to be? I can scarcely imagine what is worse than being shaved with a straight razor.

Or the thing he does next.

Jesus Christ the thing he does next. When he takes away the straight razor and comes back with a bottle of oil, I honestly consider saying my safe word. If I say it, then I can escape what I know is going to be some pretty intense tormenting. Far more intense than any ideas I had about BDSM before now. Way worse than being whipped with a switch or walked around like a dog.

But then I tell myself I'm just being silly.

Being massaged is hardly the limit of human sexual endurance. People who *do* get walked around like dogs would probably think I was crazy—though that might be because they've never met Johann Wilhelm Weir. Who rather than just rubbing it on me, decides the best course of action is to ever so slowly trail that syrupy liquid over the least-sensitive parts of my body.

Which pretty must turns them into the *most* sensitive parts of my body, immediately. Seriously, my elbow almost cries out in delight. Twice my hands nearly leave the metal—the first time because something unbearably slick and bizarrely warm eases down into a crevice I didn't know I had, and the second time because he says "Are you getting close to begging yet, or should I keep doing this for another hour or so?"

And to be honest, I just really need them free so I can kill him.

"I'm not even anywhere near. I'm totally fine."

"Is that why you're trembling like that?"

"It's just cold in here."

"I keep it at a balmy seventy degrees. Plus, I heated the oil before I started this, so you get that nice hint of heat to add to that fire currently burning under your skin."

"There's no fire burning under my skin."

"So how come your cheeks are all pink?"

"Probably the same reason yours are," I try, but as soon as I do I want to take it back. It only makes him redouble his efforts, and his efforts were pretty unbearable to begin with. After I point out that he looks just as turned on as I feel, things get much worse for me. For a start, I have to accept that I have noticed the jutting shape in his corduroy pants and deal with the great rolling wave of pleasure that pushes through me at the thought.

And then there is the slick sensation of that oil on my skin.

Only now it seems to be between my legs oh God, he just poured it between my legs. My pussy is all bare and open and he just lets it ease all over everything in thick slippery waves, until I kind of want to die. It feels like someone is licking my clit, only without the added satisfaction of pressure. It's all tease and no fulfilment, and okay yeah now I really am crying. The tears just squeeze out of my eyes before I can stop them.

I bare my teeth at him and snarl.

But he has no mercy on me.

"Is there something more you want me to do?" he asks, as though we are in a kitchen preparing for a casual dinner party. He wants to chop carrots for me and I need him to pass the peas, rather than this agonizing reality.

My clit honestly feels the size of a small bus. I can feel a miniature heartbeat pounding away inside it. And of course that heartbeat only gets harder when he makes his next offer.

"Maybe I should stroke a finger through all that mess," he says.

Then just kind of lowers his hand toward me, inch by inch. Eyes always on mine as he moves, until finally I can almost feel it. I can feel the air between his finger and my body touching me. Every nerve ending in my body is gathered in that one spot just south of my belly button, waiting and waiting and bursting with the need for him to do it.

And then he does, and oh I wish he hadn't. I had no idea there was some kind of undiscovered sex organ in that spot. I didn't know it would feel like being covered in molten lava to have him just slide through the oil that seems to have pooled there. He only makes a little circle, for God's sake. It doesn't seem fair. It doesn't seem right. My whole body is alight.

"What do you think?" he asks, but I can't answer him. I'm so close to coming that I have to use all my focus to totally pretend I'm not. I'm just going tense all over for no reason. I'm biting my lip because I have a nervous tic. My clit isn't weirdly jumping in this really delicious way, and I never make a sound.

"Maybe too much, huh?"

"No, no, I did *not* gasp just then."

"Should probably take this finger away."

"Please no, I wasn't going to do it."

"You weren't going to do what?"

"I wasn't going to come. No one comes over a finger on their belly button that's crazy—just put it back and I promise I will be completely cool about it."

"Okay I'll put it back."

"Great, awesome thank—" I start to say, but only because I am a total fool.

"After you tell me about your day."

"What?"

"Tell me about your day. How was nineteenth-century literature?"

"You're asking me about nineteenth-century literature?"

"Sure. We're a couple. We should talk about couple-y things," he says, but it's somewhat hard to take him seriously when I have silky oil running between the cheeks of my ass. When I can almost feel it sliding into me there, so lewdly it makes me a whole bunch of things happen. My clit sort of jumps over the sensation, and I know I start to shake.

And yet somehow in the middle of this I have to reason with him.

"We *do* talk about couple-y things. I love talking about couple-y things with you. But right now I think it's more the time for fondle-me-all-over," I say.

And he does. He does fondle me—so suddenly and so thoroughly it sort of takes my breath away. He just slides three fingers over my slippery mound, and of course everything just parts for him. Everything just opens up for him, from my flushed and slippery folds to the wet and wanting hole I usually need guys to work on for a bit.

But of course that is not the case here.

He simply eases those three fingers in, without having to force it all. He fucks into me, so sweetly I say his name.

And then just like that he pulls away again.

"Was that the kind of thing you had in mind or…"

"You *know* that's the kind of thing I had in mind."

"Or maybe you'd prefer it if I rubbed your clit? How about that?" he asks, and I go to answer him. I expect there to be some more back-and-forth here, before he finally gives in. Which I suppose only makes it more intense when he just slides back over my slippery pussy, and finds my tight little bud with his thumb.

And by more intense I mean: the greatest pleasure of my life. He pulls away again before I can come, but to be honest this time I can't complain. That one little gut shot of sensation was sweeter than any orgasm I've actually had. I have to bring my legs up to my stomach for it. I babble incoherently over it. Nothing beats how it makes me feel.

Except the second stroke he gives me, half an hour later. The one that comes when I'm sobbing and moaning and making up stories about my arms aching. The one that makes me thank him, even after I spent so long cursing him out for doing this to me. Two minutes ago I called him a withholding jerk, and now I'm singing his praises. "You're the best," I tell him, "you're the best."

But then he leaves me alone again.

And this time, he does it for so long I start to calm down. My body cools and at one point I doze. I even kind of think I can take anything, when he finally comes back down to give me a drink and stroke my hair and tell me how good I'm doing. "You're amazing," he tells me, and I think he really means it.

But he *also* means the little flick of his tongue over one of my nipples—just the tiniest little lick, nothing more—and once that happens I have to hate him again. I have to. Somehow that slight thing puts my body right back on high alert, even though I could have sworn I had it under control. I had everything under control and then he does one thing and I'm done for.

And he knows it. I can see it in his eyes when he sits back against the frame at the end of the bed. They are so full of amusement and surety, as though he understands me better than I understand myself. He knew it would immediately get me squirmy. He can see me drooling over his mouth. He can tell I just want him to lick.

But I think there's one thing he's overlooked.

I know him just as well.

I can see why he really went upstairs. It wasn't for me. It was for him. It was so he could calm down—because he completely has now. That urgent-looking shape is no longer between his legs. The flush in his cheeks has died down. He can just casually sit there eating a banana without a care in the world, and that gives me some pause. A lot of things he has done give me a pause, and all them make me wonder about whom is really in charge.

And whether that can change.

I think I might be able to make that change.

"I want you to lick me again," I say, and when I do I try to keep my voice calm, and neutral. Not a demand, exactly, but not just a question. Somewhere in between, where everything is nice and safe and easy.

Or so he seems to imagine.

"I think that can be arranged."

"Come on then. Come and do it."

"You can do better than that."

"*Please* come and do it."

"That you all you got?"

"I *need* you to come and do it."

"I see. And how much do you need?"

"So much. I'm burning up for it."

"Well, I guess it won't hurt," he says, and then oh then I know I have him. I just have to wait patiently for him to put the banana aside, and make a big show of crawling up the bed to me. Every move he makes so laborious I almost lose it several times.

But then finally, finally his mouth is at my breast again.

So ready to taunt, and tease, and torment me into losing my mind.

In the exact way I now am. I'm ready. I want him inside me.

And I'm going to get it, if it kills me.

"No, baby. No. Lick my clit. Lick my wet cunt. Make me come all over your face—because God knows I will. The second you press that gorgeous mouth to my hot, slippery pussy I'm just going to burst. I'm going to moan and writhe and rock against your face until you can't take a single second more. Until you just have to take me hard and fast, you have to fuck me with that big cock of yours and when you do I know you will just about split me in two. Oh man I dream about you splitting me in two," I say, and that almost does it. That careful expression slips just a bit, and though he tells me he's never going to do it I can hear the waver in his voice. I just have to push a little more.

Just a tiny bit more...

"I know you're not, because you're not really controlling my pleasure at all. You're controlling yours," I say, so pleased with myself for nailing him that I hardly expect the immediate response I get. I'm still busy basking in my victory, most of me preparing for maybe a slight denial.

But God, that makes his actual response so much sweeter. I have no time to brace myself. He gives me no quarter at all. The moment the words are out he falls on me like someone cut his strings, so ravenous for a second I scarcely keep up. Just when I think I have a handle on the fist he forces into my hair, he switches it up. He gets a handful of my ass, and squeezes so firmly it sets my flesh on fire.

And when he talks...

Does he know how he sounds when he talks?

"Gonna take you," he says, though really the word *says* seems like a stretch. He growls it out, like some animal that barely remembers what it was to be a man. I scarcely know if he really said *take* there, because his words are all one rough syllable.

But I want to believe he did.

I need to, out of deference to all the things it does to me. As soon as I hear it I get this long, thick pulse through my body, so strong I think it might pass for an orgasm. My cunt seems to clench around nothing and my clit definitely swells, which usually means something has happened. In fact, the only thing that makes me think otherwise is what happens when he gets ahold of me between my legs.

Because it gets worse.

It gets stronger. I should be replete, now, and instead I find myself arching my back. I groan long and low, in a way I never have before. It sounds like someone dying, and in point of fact, I am. I am dying of desire. My lust is like a living thing, and it pretty much destroys everything else in its path. All thoughts of decency and decorum completely go out the window, and are replaced by this writhing, moaning, desperate thing.

He sinks two fingers into me, and I gasp at him to do it harder.

I shove down on that intrusion, until he gives back just as good as he gets. He fucks me with them, over and over until that orgasm actually is upon me. Then just as it crests, he does the best possible thing he could.

He pulls away just long enough to unbutton his pants.

And roll a condom on from the drawer by his bed.

At last, I think, in one long relief-filled rush.

But then he speaks. *Turn over*, he tells me, and all of that relief disappears. It trails away, leaving me just as frustrated and on edge as I was a second before. All I can think about is what exactly he wants this for, and just how bad it is going to be. Though even with the full minute of tense thinking time he gives me, I still don't get it. I twist onto my front, thinking he will immediately fuck me.

And get the hot, hard press of his mouth between my legs. Right over the slick split of my sex, right where I am swollen and sensitive and so ready for more. All teeth and tongue and greedy kisses, until I just cannot take another second more. I sob, over the sensation it provokes. I sob and say his name and simply will not stay still.

But that's okay.

He likes it that way.

"Oh you greedy little thing," he says, voice so thick with lust it sounds obscene. It makes me shake just to hear it, and especially after he adds one more thing. "So ready for my cock, huh?" he says, and boy does he have a point.

He practically shoves into me, once the words are out.

Yet somehow I feel no pain. Everything is so slippery and so open he just glides right in, despite being just as enormous as he claimed. I honestly think I feel him in my throat for a second. My eyes go wide—though that may be more to do with the sensation.

For the first time, I fully understand what people mean when they talk about the G-spot. I thought I had it before, but nothing was ever like this. Nothing ever made me grind my teeth together and try to get away, but this absolutely does.

Because when I do, he gets a handful of my hair.

"No, no, no," he says. "Take it. Take it."

And then he pulls me back on that impossible cock. He uses that hand in my hair and another on my hip, yanking and shoving and fucking until I sort of want to let go of the bed. I have to let go of the bed. I need to claw his back somehow, even though his back is behind me. I need to pull at *his* hair, just to let him know how it feels.

Like fucking bliss.

Like the best thing ever. Oh my God I think my scalp is going to be bruised, but what the fuck do I care? It is amazing. All of this is amazing. After a couple of seconds of keeping his cool he just goes for it, and honestly nothing in my sexual experience equals that. Clearly, I have been doing it wrong for a long, long time.

Because this is right. This bloom of pleasure I get every time he fucks into me is right. It shakes me all the way through to my bones. It bores down to some secret center of me. By the time I come I am already a sweaty, moaning mess, so far gone I think I just told him to *do it in my ass*. I think I asked him to make a mess all over my face.

And then a great, wrenching wave of pleasure claims me, and I know nothing else. I am just my pussy as it clenches far too tightly around him, again and again and again, body screaming so loud I am sort of afraid to let the sound out. I have to grit my teeth around it, and allow it air only when I think it might not level a wall.

But even in its smallest form, it sounds insane. He tells me it sounds insane, in a way I would feel bad about. If he wasn't doing all the same things. I can feel him shuddering just like I did and groaning as loudly as I wanted to, and when he finally goes over it's a hurricane. He pounds me so hard my teeth rattle and holds me so close I think we merge.

All of which is good enough on its own.

Though not quite as sweet as his one last act.

He *bites* me. He bites my shoulder as his cock jerks and comes thickly inside me, so hard I know there will be a mark later. *He* knows there will be a mark later, because as soon as he comes to his senses he goes to get some ice. No moment of basking in the afterglow or pausing to catch his breath. Just ice, for the wound I barely realize I have.

I don't care. I don't even think about it. I'm too busy thanking him to understand what his concern means. To see it all over his face, like an admission of some crime he didn't even do. And by the time I do see it—by the time I understand that this is a real issue for him, of the kind people never recover from—it's far too late.

Oh it's far, far, far too late, for both of us.

I EXPECT THINGS to go out with a bang. But it's really more of a whimper. First he calls to say he has to skip our date later. Then he fails to answer a message I leave for him, about a song I heard that made me think of his face. And then after that the work is really mostly done, because my mind just does the rest.

I start to cringe, thinking of that face comment. I pick our whole relationship apart—and it isn't exactly hard. We met because I was setting his store on fire, then fell headlong into feelings over the course of a night. I was thinking he was a fellow survivor from some distant planet within hours of meeting him, for fuck's sake.

Of course it was all going to fall apart.

The biting stuff is probably not even the reason. He's just tired of me. I'm just a silly college kid, whereas he wants a wife with a real estate license and a hankering for a home in the Hamptons. He probably has big future plans about kids with cute names and garage sales and Sundays, and no matter how much of an asshole I think he is or how you twist and turn me, I'm never going to fit into that.

Of course I'm never going to fit into that.

I still have his bracelet around my wrist. The thing I liked most about him was his ability to say things out loud that everyone else keeps in their heads, and my fondest memory of our time together is smoking pot in a bath. I don't value the things normal people do, or understand what love really is.

I think it can happen that quickly.

When really it probably never happened at all.

I have to let it go—and after a while I do. It doesn't even hurt too much to do it. It hurts only when I let myself think of what we could have been. Or what I fleetingly thought we were.

But then isn't that what life is?

Fleetingly thinking everything might be wonderful, only to have it fade away? I remember when I used to think I would grow up and have a cool friend who really liked me and we would giggle and eat marshmallows and have long talks about books. And instead, I have Marnie. Who is nice and mostly good and never really horrible. But she doesn't tell me about the part in *The NeverEnding Story* that made her cry. She never asks me about what I might be reading at the moment. She isn't like him.

I never even told her about what we had.

I never told anyone, in fact.

I could have imagined him, for all the outside evidence he left behind. And in all honesty, the whole thing seems like a story someone made up. Girl gets accidentally kidnapped and falls madly in love with her captor, who just happens to be funny and kind and good and cool and into great books and is awesome in bed. I mean, I could probably label all of that reality, if you took just one of those things away. But all of them together?

I never get all of them together.

It must have been a dream.

In a few more weeks it will fade.

I just need to focus on other things—a task that proves very hard indeed at the best of times. But becomes almost impossible when I go to cross the street outside campus on one Friday evening, already soaked to the bone and so tired in my soul. So tired that when I see his car I want to cry, but God knows I keep it inside.

I walk slowly to the passenger door.

I stay calm, the way his future real estate wife would.

And when he tells me to get in, I do barely anything. I sit and I let the warmth and the silence wash over me, but I don't turn and look his way.

Not even when he says:

"I just couldn't leave it like that."

Two weeks ago I would have been relieved.

But not now. Not after so long. Instead, I am stone.

"Leave it like what? It's not a big deal," I say, and even manage a shrug. A really, really convincing shrug, that completely shows how much I do not care.

Or at least it would, to anyone else in the history of existence.

"Yeah, apart from the fact that you just said it's not a big deal like you've died inside," he says, and then I think I die inside some more.

Still, though, I refuse to admit it.

I keep looking straight ahead, at the rain making patterns on the glass.

"Wow, someone thinks a lot of themselves."

"No, no, it's more that *I* feel like I've died inside, and seeing as how you're pretty much my soul mate I'm going to go ahead and imagine you're feeling the same," he says, and when he does I almost look. The need to do it swells up inside me, and I barely resist. My resolve is eroding, bit by bit, and when he adds more another chunk of it goes. "Only you want to hide that fact because I kept fobbing you off like a total asshole, instead of just explaining what the problem was."

"You don't have to explain about the house you want in the Hamptons."

"What house I want in the Hamptons?"

"You know, the one you want to have with a woman who sells real estate instead of some silly college kid who wanted to play sex games."

"I don't think silly college kids who just wanted to play sex games would manage to nail me harder than anyone I've ever met," he says, and after he does something shifts. Suddenly I want to crack a joke, instead of barely responding.

"I think technically *you* nailed me *really* hard."

And I am so glad I do. Once I have, that shift becomes seismic. I see his hands make fists on the wheel, and when he speaks again his voice actually cracks.

"I meant psychologically speaking, not how viciously I—" he starts, but then a chasm seems to open up in his sentence and swallows the rest whole. Hell, I think the chasm swallows *me* whole, because honestly I just cannot believe him. I cannot believe me.

We are both the most ridiculous people alive.

Him, for really thinking that mattered.

And me for wondering if it was anything else.

"Oh my God is that really all it was? Just an insane aversion to fucking me like a maniac?" I ask, so full of disbelief I think I could rival him in the incredulous Olympics.

Not that he appreciates my efforts at all.

I think he gives me a four point two.

"You say that like it means nothing."

"It *does* mean nothing."

"Not to me. I don't want to be that guy."

"*Which* guy? The awesome one that I am totally in love with?" I ask, yet still he refuses to get it. I just laid my ass on the line there, and this is what he comes out with:

"The one who loses control."

"I *like* it when you lost control," I say.

But he just shakes his head.

"I didn't. I don't. I hate it. I like being cool and calm and steady. That's how a guy with my proclivities is supposed to be. Not grabbing women because they set fire to his store. Not leaving bruises when I fuck you. Not fucking full stop—I want to just make love," he says, and sounds so wistful I actually consider strangling him.

The only thing that stops me is the knowledge that he really doesn't understand.

"You *did* make love to me, you idiot," I say, and this time I look at him when I do. It sort of hurts my eyes to, but I can take it. I can do this, because that sound I hear in the distance is almost certainly his heart.

And I don't think it beats for anyone but me.

"Are you serious?"

"Absolutely. Do you really think making love is just about, like, soft music and crying in the rain and satin sheets? Man, for a sexually adventurous guy you sure are close minded," I say—much to his withering disgust. Seriously, he looks like I just insulted his grandmother.

But boy, am I ever glad I did.

I can hear that heart now, like coming thunder.

"I am *not*. I just don't like being rough."

"No, you don't like the idea of me not liking it. Or maybe of breaking me—but you won't. You have to trust me now when I say you won't. I'm not made of china. I won't come apart because you pounded me."

"I know that."

"Then act like it. Be with me," I say, then brace myself.

Even though I know I don't need to. I know it before he answers.

Though it makes my own heart thunder in kind, when he does.

"I don't ever want to do anything else. I tried. It was hopeless."

"I know. My life without German stories and mild bondage sucked."

"Who am I supposed to discuss seventies music with?"

"No one can spin theories about 'Cecilia' like I can."

"And baths have just not been the same," he says, and that seals it.

"So what are you waiting for, wolf? A message from our home planet? Because I've got news for you: no message is coming. We are the only ones left. The sole survivors of some distant place, where people like talking about books and being in baths and saying out loud all the things you usually keep to yourself. All those thoughts I have to hide from everyone else, and never do with you. I want you to never have to with me."

"Then let me start now with the only thing I think I ever kept to myself: I want you more than I've ever wanted anyone. All the time, every day, every moment I spend with you, I am consumed by my own desire. Never think otherwise just because I do my best to be tender and say *love* before *lust*. Both things are there in me, more than they ever have been for anyone else," he says, as he takes my hand. As he kisses my mouth, so soft to start and so fierce to finish. My wolf, I think. My secret werewolf.

"And if you'll let me, I'll show you all the ways I can be."

Epilogue

MY FAVORITE GAME is *the forest*, though I have no idea why we call it that. It has almost nothing to do with trees and undergrowth and almost everything to do with what fun we have in it. He says run, and then I have to run. I have to dash between branches and leap over logs, heart ever in my mouth for something I never fear in real life.

In our real life, I come home from a long day at the library, full of stories about the research we did that day. And he will wrap me in his arms and show me some old book or play me something cool while I sink into a bath. He might trim his beard while I'm in there, or maybe join me for a soak. Say that he's glad I seem so happy.

Or tell me that he is too.

Just like ordinary couples do.

Because we are in every way, except maybe for this one. The one where I run. I can hear him now behind me, so loud it drowns out everything else. It obliterates all memory of him as my loving husband, and instead lets me think of the wolf. My wolf chasing me through the woods, so eager to catch me that he barely thinks about how fragile I am.

Everything is just the rough-and-tumble when he finally does, the feel of his mouth against my throat, so full of teeth. The smell of him and the size of him and his hands, so eager to pin me down now. Oh God, so eager to pin me down.

Sometimes I think he might never let me back up again—but if that was so, I would be okay. After all, there is nowhere I would rather live my life. No place I would rather be.

His fierce, frightening, loving, and loyal arms are the only ones I need around me.

CHARLOTTE STEIN is the acclaimed author of over thirty short stories, novellas, and novels, including the recently DABWAHA-nominated *Run to You*. When not writing deeply emotional and intensely sexy books, she can be found eating jelly turtles, watching terrible sitcoms, and occasionally lusting after hunks. For more on Charlotte, visit www.charlottestein.net.

Discover great authors, exclusive offers, and more at hc.com.